Ben Jonson's The Devil is an Ass: A Retelling

David Bruce

Published by David Bruce, 2022.

BEN JONSON'S THE DEVIL IS AN ASS: A RETELLING

First edition. July 10, 2022.

Copyright © 2022 David Bruce.

ISBN: 979-8201984021

Written by David Bruce.

Table of Contents

Cover Photograph for *The Devil is an Ass*:
https://pixabay.com/photos/costume-cute-demon-devil-evil-15829/

Educate Yourself
Read Like A Wolf Eats
Be Excellent to Each Other
Books Then, Books Now, Books Forever

***

In this retelling, as in all my retellings, I have tried to make the work of literature accessible to modern readers who may lack the knowledge about mythology, religion, and history that the literary work's contemporary audience had.

Do you know a language other than English? If you do, I give you permission to translate this book, copyright your translation, publish or self-publish it, and keep all the royalties for yourself. (Do give me credit, of course, for the original retelling.)

I would like to see my retellings of classic literature used in schools, so I give permission to the country of Finland (and all other countries) to buy one copy of this eBook and give copies to all students forever. I also give permission to the state of Texas (and all other states) to buy one copy of this eBook and give copies to all students forever. I also give permission to all teachers to buy one copy of this eBook and give copies to all students forever.

Teachers need not actually teach my retellings. Teachers are welcome to give students copies of my eBooks as background material. For example, if they are teaching Homer's *Iliad* and *Odyssey*, teachers are welcome to give students copies of my *Virgil's* Aeneid: *A Retelling in Prose* and tell students, "Here's another ancient epic you may want to read in your spare time."

CAST OF CHARACTERS

SATAN *the great devil*

PUG *the less devil (an imp)*

INIQUITY *the Vice*. The Vice was a stock character, often comic, in medieval morality plays. The Vice's job was supposed to be to tempt people to do evil. The Vice accompanied Satan. At the time of Ben Jonson's play, the Vice is an old-fashioned, out-of-date character.

FABIAN FITZDOTTREL *a squire of Norfolk (a dotterel is a foolish bird)*

MISTRESS FRANCES FITZDOTTREL *his wife. "Mistress" means "female head of the house." She was the mistress or lady-boss of the servants — or servant — in the household. Her husband sometimes calls her "wedlock," which is appropriate because her marriage is a form of imprisonment.*

MERECRAFT *the projector ("mere" means "solely," "completely," or "only"; "crafty" means "tricky" in an unethical sense). A projector comes up with moneymaking schemes; projectors need money to put into effect their moneymaking schemes. Merecraft is a con man.*

EVERILL *his champion and defender. Everill gets Merecraft access to wealthy men to defraud. Everill is a con man.*

WITTIPOL *a young gallant. "Wit" means intelligence, and "pol" means "head" or "parrot." The name is ambiguous, so readers will have to study his character to see whether he is an intelligent man or merely an intelligent parrot. Even an intelligent parrot is not very intelligent.*

EUSTACE MANLY *his friend. Manly is a good and ethical man.*

ENGINE *a broker (a middleman; an engine is a piece of trickery). Engine is a con man.*

TRAINS *the projector's (Merecraft's) manservant (a train is a lure or a bait)*

GILTHEAD *a goldsmith (a gilthead is a fish with gold markings on its head)*

PLUTARCHUS *his son*

SIR PAUL EITHERSIDE *a lawyer and Justice (lawyers can argue for either side: prosecution or defense)*

LADY EITHERSIDE *his wife*

LADY TAILBUSH *the lady projectress*

PITFALL *her female attendant (a pitfall is a trap)*

AMBLER *her gentleman usher*
SLEDGE *a blacksmith, the constable*
SHACKLES *jail keeper of Newgate prison*
SERGEANTS
Four JAIL KEEPERS
Three WAITERS
The Scene
London
Notes
In this culture, a man of higher rank would use words such as "thee," "thy," "thine," and "thou" to refer to a servant. However, two close friends or a husband and wife could properly use "thee," "thy," "thine," and "thou" to refer to each other.

The word "sirrah" is a term usually used to address a man of lower social rank than the speaker. This was socially acceptable, but sometimes the speaker would use the word as an insult when speaking to a man whom he did not usually call "sirrah." Close friends, whether male or female, could also call each other "sirrah."

A purse is used to carry money. Men carried what they called a purse.

The word "wench" in Ben Jonson's time was not necessarily negative. It was often used affectionately.

The events of *The Devil is an Ass* take place in one day.

CHAPTER 1
— 1.1 —

Satan and Pug, a minor devil, talked together in London. Pug had made a request to Satan that Satan was now laughing at. They were visiting earth, and Pug wanted to take possession of a body and stay there for a while.

"Ho, ho, ho, ho, ho, ho, ho, ho," Satan laughed. "To earth? And why do thou want to go to earth, thou foolish spirit? What would thou do on earth?"

"I want to go to earth to do, great chief, that which time shall show you," Pug said. "I am asking only for my month on earth, which every petty, puny devil has. Within that length of time, the Court of Hell will hear something that may gain me a longer grant of time, perhaps, to spend on earth."

Satan said, "For doing what?

"Laming a poor cow or two?

"Entering a sow to make her bear prematurely her farrow?

"Or somewhere between this place and the village of Tottenham crossing the path of a market-woman's mare and diverting it from its destination?"

The village of Tottenham was only a few miles from London.

Satan continued, "These are your usual main achievements, Pug.

"You must have some plot now concerning the storing of ale in casks: You want to make the yeast stale.

"Or you want to manage the churn so that the butter doesn't form, despite the housewife's cord, or her hot spit. You want to keep the housewife's cord or her hot spit from making butter."

In this society, housewives believed that wrapping a cord around a churn or thrusting a hot spit into the cream would encourage the formation of butter.

Satan continued, "Or some good ribibe — old hag — about Kentish Town or Hoxton, in the area of north London, you would hang now for a witch because she will not let you play round Robin?"

Puck, in William Shakespeare's *A Midsummer Night's Dream*, is also known as Robin Goodfellow. He goes around and plays tricks such as some of the ones Satan says that Pug likes to perform. Puck's tricks are annoying, but they are not life threatening.

Satan continued, "And you'll go sour a citizen's cream in preparation for Sunday, so that she may be accused of it, and condemned by a Middlesex jury, to the satisfaction of their offended friends, the Londoners' wives, whose teeth were set on edge with it?"

Middlesex juries had a well-deserved reputation for severity.

Satan continued, "Foolish fiend, stay in your place, know your own strengths, and don't go beyond the sphere of your activity. You are too dull, stupid, and foolish a devil to be trusted out in those parts, Pug, upon any affair that may concern our name on earth. It is not everyone's work. The state of Hell must care whom it employs in point of reputation, here about London.

"You would make, I think, an agent to be sent to Lancashire properly enough, or some parts of Northumberland, as long as you would have good instructions, Pug."

In other words, Pug could do good work in Lancashire or in Northumberland, but not in and around London, which is just too evil for an imp like Pug to deal with.

"Oh, chief!" Pug said. "You do not know, dear chief, what is in me.

"Test me for just a fortnight, or for a week, and lend me only a Vice to carry with me and help me corrupt any playfellow, and you will see that there will come more out of it than you'll imagine, precious chief."

A Vice was a companion of devils such as Satan. They had various names, which were the names of specific moral vices.

"What Vice?" Satan asked. "What kind of Vice would thou have?"

"Why, any," Pug said. "Let the Vice be Fraud, or Covetousness, or Lady Vanity.

"Or old Iniquity — I'll call him here."

He called, "Iniquity!"

Iniquity the Vice appeared and said, "Who is he who calls upon me, and would seem to lack a Vice? Before his words are half spoken, I am with him in a trice, and here, there, and everywhere, as the cat is with the mice. I am true *vetus Iniquitas*."

Iniquity the Vice knew Latin: *Vetus Iniquitas* is Latin for "old Inequity."

The word "iniquity" means "gross injustice" or "wickedness."

Iniquity the Vice said, "Do thou lack cards, friend, or dice? I will teach thee to cheat, child, to swindle and cheat, lie, and swagger, and forever and at once to be drawing forth thy dagger.

"I will teach thee to swear by Gog's nowns — by God's wounds — like a Lusty Juventus — like a Pleasure-Seeking Young Man.

"You will wear a cloak down to thy heel, and a hat like a penthouse, aka awning, Thy breeches will have three fingers of padding, and thy jacket will be all belly because it is stuffed with bombast — stuffing.

"And you will be with a wench who shall feed thee with aphrodisiacal cock-stones that are found in the gizzards of roosters — this wench will also feed thee with jelly."

Iniquity the Vice skipped with delight.

Pug said to Satan, "Isn't it excellent, chief? How nimble he is!"

Iniquity the Vice said, "Child of Hell, this is nothing! I will perform a leap from the top of the steeple of St. Paul's Cathedral" — Iniquity the Vice was out of touch because lightning-caused fire had destroyed the steeple in 1561, and the current year was 1616 — "to the Standard, an ornamental pillar in Cheapside, and lead thee a dance through the streets without fail, as if I were a high-quality needle made in Spain, with a thread at my tail."

Spanish lovers had a red-hot reputation, and readers can guess the meaning of a Spanish "needle." (Non-metaphorical Spanish needles also had a reputation for good quality.)

The tail was the Vice's bottom, and the non-metaphorical thread was his devil's tail.

Iniquity the Vice now described a journey through disreputable areas of London, such as those filled with prostitutes, thieves, pubs, and lawyers:

"We will survey the suburbs, and make forth our sallies —

"We will go down Petticoat Lane and up the Smock Alleys — those haunts of prostitutes —

"We will go to Shoreditch, which is known for prostitutes; Whitechapel, which is known for thieves; and so continue on to St. Katherine's precinct, which is known for pubs — we will drink with the alcohol-loving Dutch there, and take away from there their patterns for weaving.

"From thence we will put in at Custom House Quay and see how the mercantile agents and apprentices play false with their masters; and geld —

lighten — many a full pack, to spend it on pies at the Dagger and the Woolsack taverns."

The mercantile agents and apprentices would steal items to sell to make money to spend on pies.

"Brave, brave Iniquity!" Pug said.

He then asked Satan, "Won't this do, chief?"

Iniquity the Vice said:

"Boy, I will bring thee to the bawds and the roisterers feasting with claret wine and oysters at Billingsgate.

"From thence we will use oars to shoot boats upstream through the narrow arch-supports of the London Bridge, child, to go to the Cranes in the Vintry — three cranes used to upload wine from boats — and see there the gimlets that are used for piercing casks of wine, and see how they make their entry!

"Or if thou had rather go down to the Strand, in time to watch as the lawyers come dabbled — they dabble in law — from Westminster Hall, and observe closely how they cling with their clients together. As ivy is to oak, so velvet is to leather."

The lawyers wore velvet, and the clients wore leather.

Iniquity the Vice concluded, "Ha, boy, the things I would show thee!"

"Splendid!" Pug said. "Splendid!"

Satan said to Iniquity the Vice, "Be quiet, dotard!"

He then said to Pug, "And thou more ignorant thing, who so admires Iniquity the Vice, are thou the spirit thou seem to be? Are thou so poor and misguided that thou choose this for a Vice to advance the cause of Hell now, as vice stands this present year?

"Remember what number this year is: six hundred and sixteen."

The year was 1616, but Satan did not want to number years using "A.D.," which is an abbreviation of the Latin *"Anno Domini,"* which means "In the year of Our Lord."

Satan was missing a thousand years in his reckoning.

Revelation 20:1-3 states this (King James Version):

1 And I saw an angel come down from heaven, having the key of the bottomless pit and a great chain in his hand.

2 And he laid hold on the dragon, that old serpent, which is the Devil, and Satan, and bound him a thousand years,

3 And cast him into the bottomless pit, and shut him up, and set a seal upon him, that he should deceive the nations no more, till the thousand years should be fulfilled: and after that he must be loosed a little season.

Most Christian authorities would say that these thousand years of imprisonment have not yet occurred, for they occur after the Second Coming of Christ.

Satan continued, "Had the number but been five hundred, though some sixty above — that's fifty years gone, and six —"

He meant the year 560, although that year was actually 1560 A.D. From 616 take away 56, and you have 560. In the year 1560, the theatrical characters known as Vices were popular on the stage in England. By 1616, these characters were old fashioned.

Satan continued, "Back then, when every great man had his Vice stand by him — the Vice wearing a long coat and shaking his wooden dagger — I could consent that then this your grave choice might have done, with his lord chief, that which most of his chamber can do now. Back then, a Vice could be an effective diabolical companion.

"But Pug, as the times now are, who is it who will receive thee? What company will you go to, or whom will thou mix with?

"Where can thou carry the Vice, except to taverns? In a tavern, the Vice will stand on a joint-stool with a Jew's harp, in order to put down and defeat the improvisatory jester Cokeley, and such performances must be before ordinary citizens. He never will be admitted there where Vennar comes."

Richard Vennar announced that a new play would be performed on 6 November 1602 at the Swan Theater; he collected the admission money to see the play and then disappeared without having the play performed. According to Satan, Iniquity the Vice may be able to compete against the jester Cokeley in modest venues, but never could he compete against a con man such as Vennar, who operated in better venues.

Satan continued:

"Iniquity the Vice may perhaps, at the end of a sheriff's dinner, skip with a rhyme on the table from new nothing — sing a doggerel song about nothing new — and take his almain — dancing — leap into a giant custard. This shall make my Lady Mayoress and her sisters laugh with all their French hoods over their shoulders."

The Fool of the Lord Mayor of London would traditionally leap into a large bowl of custard as part of the entertainment at some feasts.

Satan continued:

"But this kind of thing is not what will do to accomplish the purposes of Hell.

"There are other things that are received now upon earth for Vices. There are stranger, and newer, Vices — and they are changed every hour.

"The newer Vices ride the older Vices like they ride their horses off their legs, and the older Vices come here to Hell, whole legions of them, every week, tired and exhausted."

According to Satan, Vices such as old Iniquity could no longer compete with the new Vices that were appearing in London. The competition to commit vice had grown so fierce that Hell struggled to keep up.

Satan continued:

"We still strive to breed and rear up new Hell-Vices for Londoners, but the new Hell-Vices do not stand tall when they come to London. The Londoners turn our new Hell-Vices upside down and on our hands, and it is feared that the Londoners have a stud of their own that will put down ours."

Satan was punning bawdily. The noun "a stand" means "an erection" and the verb "to stand" means "to have an erection." The new Hell-Vices were impotent against the Londoners and their London-Vices.

Satan continued:

"Both our breed and trade will suddenly decay and dwindle unless we prevent it. Unless our Hell-Vice is a Vice of Quality or of Fashion now, the Londoners will not take it from us.

"Cart-men have gotten into the use of yellow starch, and chimney-sweepers have gotten into the use of their tobacco and strong waters: the strong ale known as hum, and mead, and obarni, which is scalded mead."

A woman named Anne Turner introduced the use of yellow starch to England. In 1615, she was tried for complicity in the murder of Sir Thomas Overbury. Found guilty, she was forced to wear yellow ruffs at her execution, at which she confessed that the devil had possessed her.

Satan continued:

"We must therefore aim at sending extraordinarily subtle Hell-Vices now, when we send a Vice to London, to keep us up in credit. We must not send old Iniquities!"

Satan said to Iniquity the Vice, "Get you back all the way to Hell, sir. Return to the making of your rope of sand again."

No one can make a rope out of sand; attempting to do so is meaningless work.

The punishments in Hell often consist of meaningless work, as these two punishments show:

1) The fifty sons of Aegyptus wanted to marry the fifty daughters of Danaus. Danaus was suspicious of Aegyptus and his fifty sons, so he fled with his fifty daughters, but Aegyptus and his fifty sons pursued them. To avoid a battle, Danaus told his fifty daughters to marry the fifty sons of Aegyptus, but although he allowed the marriages to be performed he also ordered his fifty daughters to kill the fifty sons of Aegyptus. All of his daughters except Hypermnestra, who had married Lynceus, obeyed. Hypermnestra spared Lynceus because he treated her with respect and did not force her to have sex with him their first night together. The gods did not like what the forty-nine women who had killed their husbands had done, and so those forty-nine daughters are punished in the Land of the Dead with meaningless work. They are condemned to spend all their time trying to fill up with water a container that has a big leak and so can never be filled. Only one daughter avoided this eternal punishment.

2) When Sisyphus was on his deathbed, he ordered his wife not to give his corpse a funeral. After his death, his spirit went to the Land of the Dead and complained to Pluto, King of the Dead, that he had not yet had a funeral. Pluto allowed him to return to the Land of the Living so that he could tell his wife to give him a funeral, but once he was back in the Land of the Living, he refused to return to the Land of the Dead. He lived to an advanced old age and then died again. Now he is forced to forever roll a boulder up a hill. Just as he reaches the top of the hill, he loses control of the boulder and it rolls back to the bottom of the hill again. Sisyphus can never accomplish this task, which has no value, and so his punishment is endless meaningless work.

Satan continued speaking to Iniquity the Vice:

"You are not for the Londoners' manners, nor the Londoners' times.

"They have their Vices there in London that are very similar to Virtues. You cannot tell them apart by any difference. They wear the same clothes, eat the same food, sleep in the same beds, ride in those coaches — or, very likely, four horses in a coach — as the best men and women.

"Tissue gowns, garters, and the shoe decorations known as roses, which are worth fourscore pound a pair, embroidered stockings, cut-work smocks and shirts — all of these are more certainly marks of lechery and pride now, than ever they were of true nobility!"

Religious people preached sermons against lechery and pride, both of which are deadly sins.

They also preached sermons against extravagant clothing and starch, including yellow starch. Tissue gowns were expensive — tissue cloth looked like cloth of gold. Roses were ornaments on the tops of shoes. Cut-work was elaborate embroidery with pieces of cloth cut out.

At one time in London, only the nobles wore such expensive clothing — laws of the time forbade wearing clothing designated for those above one's station in life. But now, in 1616, because of the sinful nature of the Londoners, even the drivers of carts had been using yellow starch. Previously, you could separate the nobles and the common people in London, but now that was difficult. Previously, you could separate the vices and the virtues in London, but now that was difficult — often, what seemed to be a virtue turned out to be a vice.

Iniquity the Vice bowed his head in shame and exited.

Satan then said, "But Pug, since you burn with such desire to do the commonwealth of Hell some service, I am content that you assume a body, go to earth, and visit men for one day.

"But you must take a ready-made body, Pug. I can create you none. Creation is not reserved for devils such as me.

"Nor shall you form yourself an airy body, for instead you must become subject to all impressions of the flesh you take so far as human frailty. You will be able to feel pain.

"So, there is a handsome cutpurse to be hanged at Tyburn this morning. Once his spirit has departed, you may enter his body.

"As for clothes, employ your credit with the hangman, or let our tribe of brokers furnish you with clothing."

Pug would go to earth and take possession of a naked dead body. He could get clothing from the hangman, part of whose compensation was the clothing of the people he hanged, or he could go to a pawnbroker, a member of a profession closely associated with Hell. Or he could find a third way to get clothing.

Satan continued:

"And see how far your subtlety can work through those organs; with that body, spy among mankind — you cannot there lack vices to spy upon, and therefore the less need you have to carry Vices with you. But as you make your soon-to-come early-at-night's relation of your day to us, we will listen and if we shall find it merits reward from the state of Hell, you shall have both trust and employment from us."

Satan was using the majestic plural.

"Most gracious chief!" Pug said.

"Only this much more do I bind you," Satan said. "You must serve the first man whom you meet — and that man I'll show you now."

A mortal man named Fitzdottrel walked near them.

Satan continued:

"Observe him. Yonder is the man whom you shall see first, after you find some clothing to wear.

"Follow him. But once you are engaged to serve him, there you must stay and be fixed in that job, and not shift to any other employment until the midnight's cock crows."

"I agree to any conditions so long as I can be gone!" Pug said.

"Leave, then," Satan said.

Satan and Pug exited.

— 1.2 —

Fitzdottrel, who was holding a picture of a devil, really wanted to see a devil. He had been trying to get help from occultists to do just that.

He said to himself, "Aye, they do now name Bretnor, as before they talked of Gresham, and of Doctor Forman, Franklin, and Fiske, and Savory — he was in on the murder, too — but there's not one of these who ever could yet show a man the Devil in his true form."

These people were con men, astrologers, and quacks. Some of them were connected with the murder of Sir Thomas Overbury, who was poisoned in 1613. Anne Turner, who introduced the use of yellow starch in England, was executed in connection with that murder. Franklin was the apothecary who supplied the poison that killed Sir Thomas Overbury.

Fitzdottrel continued, "They have their crystals, I know, and rings, and virgin parchment, and their dead men's skulls, their ravens' wings, their candles, and pentacles with characters — I have seen all these."

Charms were written on parchment; the skins of newborn lambs and kids (baby goats) are used to make virgin parchment. A pentacle is a pentagram; mystical characters were inscribed on pentagrams.

Fitzdottrel continued, "But — I wish that I might see the Devil! I would give a hundred of these pictures to see him once out in person and not in a picture."

He looked at the picture of a devil and then said, "May I prove to be a cuckold, a man with an unfaithful wife — and that's the one main mortal thing I fear — if I don't begin now to think that the painters have only made up the Devil and that devils don't really exist.

"By God's light, the Devil would have been seen at one time or another if he really existed.

"The Devil would not let an antique gentleman of as good a family as most are now in England — because King James I sells titles for money — run wild and call upon him thus in vain, as I have done this past year."

Fitzdottrel was an "antique" gentleman in the sense that the Fitzdottrels were a long-standing family of the gentle class.

He continued, "If the Devil does not at all exist, then why are there conjurers who say that they can summon devils? If they are not truly conjurors, then why are there laws against them? The best artists — learned men — of Cambridge, Oxford, Middlesex, and of London, Essex, and Kent, I have had in pay to raise the Devil these fifty weeks, and yet the Devil has not appeared. By God's death, I shall suspect the conjurors can make circles only shortly — small circles made for only a short time — and know only his hard names."

The conjurors had failed to summon the Devil. Why? Perhaps the circles they made around themselves for protection against the Devil they tried to summon were too small, or perhaps the conjurors gave up too quickly. Also, perhaps they lacked knowledge. Perhaps they knew only the names of the Devil — lists of these names were available — and lacked the other, specialized knowledge that a real conjuror possessed.

Fitzdottrel continued, "They say that the Devil will meet a man in person who has a mind to him. If he would do so, I have a mind and a half for him. By God's light, he should not be long absent.

"I pray to thee, the Devil, come — I long for thee!

"If I were with child by him, and my wife, too, I could not long for thee more.

"Come, yet, good Beelzebub!"

Beelzebub was one of the Devil's many names. "Good" is an adjective not normally applied to Satan.

Fitzdottrel continued, "If he were a kind Devil, and had humanity in him, he would come just to satisfy one's longing.

"I would treat him well, I swear, and I would treat him with respect, if he were to test me.

"I would not treat him as the conjurers do when they have raised him. They put him in bonds, and send him posthaste on errands a thousand miles in distance. That is preposterous, and, I believe, that is the true reason he does not come. And he has good reason. Who would be bound, who might live freely, as he may do?

"I swear all the conjurors are wrong. The burnt child dreads the fire. They do not know to treat the Devil and keep him in service. I would so welcome him, observe his diet, get him his own chamber that is decorated with wall hangings — two of them — in my own house, lend him my wife's embroidered pillows, and as I am an honest man, I think, if he had a mind to my wife, too, I would grant her to him, to make our friendship perfect. I would not do that for every man.

"I wish that the Devil would just hear me now, and would come to me in a brave young shape, and would take me at my word!

"Ha! Who is this?"

Pug walked over to Fitzdottrel. Pug had possessed the body of the recently hanged handsome young cutpurse, and he was now dressed in a fine new suit.

Pug said, "Sir, I beg your good pardon for my thus presuming upon your privacy. I was born a gentleman, I am a younger brother, and I am in some disgrace now with my friends and need some little means to keep me upright, until things can be reconciled. May it please you to let my service be of use to you, sir."

The bulk of an inheritance passed to the oldest son, and so a younger son, who was the oldest son's brother, was often left with little wealth.

Pug was asking Fitzdottrel to employ him — to put him in service.

"Service?" Fitzdottrel said to himself. "Before Hell, my heart was at my mouth until I had viewed his shoes well, for those roses on his shoes were big enough to hide a cloven foot."

Fitzdottrel had just asked the Devil to appear, and Pug had appeared, and so Fitzdottrel at first thought that Pug was the Devil, especially because the Devil was thought to have cloven feet that could be covered by the large roses that Pug was wearing on his feet.

Fitzdottrel carefully looked again at Pug's feet to see if he could tell whether they were cloven. They weren't, but Pug will explain that the Devil's — and the devils' — cloven feet are just a myth.

"No, friend, my number of servants is full," Fitzdottrel said to Pug. "I have one servant, who is my all, indeed, and does everything from the broom to the brush, for just so far I trust him. He is my wardrobe man, buyer of provisions, cook, butler, and steward; he looks after my horse, and helps to watch my wife. He has all the places that I can think of, from the garret downward even to the manger and the curry-comb for currying horses. My one servant does all of that."

"Sir, I shall put Your Worship to no charge other than my food, and as for my food I eat only a very little," Pug said. "I'll serve you for your friendship."

Pug was offering to work for no wages, but only food. He did not ask for shelter because he was authorized to be on earth and out of Hell for only one day.

"Ha?" Fitzdottrel said. "You will work without wages? I'd hearken in my ear, if I were at leisure. But now I'm busy. Please, friend, forgive me. If thou had been a devil, I would say somewhat more to thee. Thou are hindering now my meditations."

"Sir, I am a devil," Pug said.

"What!" Fitzdottrel said.

"I am a true devil, sir."

"Nay, now you lie — under your favor, friend, for I'll not quarrel," Fitzdottrel said.

This society had rules regarding duels. Normally, being called a liar meant challenging the person who called you a liar to duel. But using the phrase "under your favor" and using the word "friend" qualified the assertion enough that a challenge to duel need not be issued.

Fitzdottrel said, "I looked at your feet earlier; you cannot trick me. Your shoe's not cloven, sir, you are whole hoofed. Devils have cloven hooves."

Fitzdottrel looked at Pug's feet again.

"Sir, that's a popular error that deceives many," Pug said. "But I am what I tell you I am: I am a devil."

"What's your name?"

"My name is Devil, sir."

"Is what you are saying true?"

"Indeed, it is, sir."

"By God's eyelid!" Fitzdottrel said. "There's some omen in this! What part of the country are you from?"

"I am from Derbyshire, sir, about the Peak Cavern," Pug said.

"That hole belonged to your ancestors?"

"Yes, it is called the Devil's Arse, sir."

Fitzdottrel said to himself, "I'll employ him for the namesake, and I will turn away my other manservant, and save four pounds a year by doing that! There's luck, and thrift, too! The Devil himself may come hereafter as well."

He said to Pug, "Friend, I receive you into my service. But first I must inform you of this beforehand: If you offend me, I must beat you. It is a kind of exercise I am accustomed to use, and I cannot be without it."

"Yes, if I do not offend, then you can follow your rule, certainly," Pug said.

If he never offended, he would never be beaten, and so Pug was OK with Fitzdottrel following that rule.

"Indeed, Devil, I will follow my rule very heartily!" Fitzdottrel said. "I'll call you by your surname, because I love it."

Wittipol, Manly, and Engine talked together. Wittipol was a young gallant, Manly was his friend, and Engine was a middleman or broker. Engine was carrying a cloak.

Engine said to Wittipol, "Yonder Fitzdottrel walks, sir. I'll go lift him for you."

The phrase "lift him" meant 1) "make him excited in emotion" and 2) "excite his pride." In addition, "lift" is a pun because some engines do the work of lifting.

"To him, good Engine, raise him up by degrees, gently, and hold him there, too," Wittipol said. "You can do it. Show yourself now a mathematical — exact and calculating — broker."

"I'll warrant you that I will for half a piece," Engine said.

A piece is a gold coin worth 22 shillings.

"It is done, sir," Wittipol said. "Half a piece, it is."

Engine took Fitzdottrel aside and spoke to him.

Manly asked, "Is it possible that there should be such a man?"

Engine and Wittipol were trying to persuade Fitzdottrel to do something that most husbands would never consider doing.

"You shall be your own witness," Wittipol said. "I'll not labor to tempt you past your faith."

In other words, Manly would see the evidence for himself that yes, such a man exists; there was no need for Wittipol to persuade him that such a man exists. That kind of persuasion could result in a trial of faith, including faith that men are basically good.

"And is his wife so very beautiful, do you say?" Manly asked.

"I have not seen her since I came home from travel, and they say she is not altered," Wittipol said. "According to other people, she still looks the same as when I left. Back then, before I went, I saw her only once; but even so, she has stayed always in my mind's eye — no object has removed her."

"Beauty is a fair guest, friend," Manly said, "and once lodged deep in the eyes, she hardly leaves the inn. How does her husband, Fitzdottrel, keep her?"

"He keeps her very finely dressed," Wittipol said. "However sordid he himself is, he is sensual that way. In every dressing he studies her."

Fitzdottrel carefully looked at his wife in each outfit she wore, and he may have carefully studied her each time she dressed.

The word "sordid" means "dirty" or "mean." Certainly, Fitzdottrel overvalued money in some areas of his life. As we have seen, he paid his one servant only four pounds a year. In other areas of his life, however, such as his wife's clothing, he was willing to spend money.

"And he furnishes himself from the brokers?" Manly asked.

A broker was a middleman in bargains; for example, some people would go to a broker and pawn fine clothing. For special occasions, Fitzdottrel rented fine clothes for himself. He was willing to spend much money to dress himself well.

"Yes," Wittipol said, "that's a hired suit he now has on in order to see the play *The Devil is an Ass* today. This man named Engine gets three or four pounds a week by him. Fitzdottrel dares not miss a new play or a feast, whatever the rate he has to pay for hired clothes, and he thinks that he himself is still new in other men's old."

The clothing he wore may have been other men's old clothing, but the clothing was new to Fitzdottrel.

"But wait," Manly said, thinking about the feasts Fitzdottrel attended. "Does he love food so much?"

"Truly, he does not hate it," Wittipol said. "But that's not it. His belly and his palate would be compounded with for reason — he puts other priorities before his appetite. Indeed, he has an intelligence of that strange credit with him as opposed to all other men, as it makes him do just what it wishes. This strange obsession ravishes him forth wherever it pleases, to any assembly or place, and would make him conclude that he is ruined should he miss one public meeting because of the belief he has of his own great and catholic — universal and all-encompassing — strengths in arguing and discourse."

Fitzdottrel attended feasts but not because of the food. He had convinced himself that he was a very intelligent man and a fine persuasive speaker, and that was why he attended so many public meetings and assemblies.

Engine had persuaded Fitzdottrel to try on the cloak.

"My plot is working, I see," Wittipol said. "Fitzdottrel has got the cloak on him."

Fitzdottrel said to Engine, "This is a fair garment, I swear by my faith, Engine!"

"It was never made, sir, for under threescore pounds, I assure you," Engine said.

Any assurance made by Engine ought not to be reassuring: He was a con man.

Engine continued, "It will yield thirty pounds if sold."

Threescore pounds is sixty pounds. Engine meant that the cloak could be worn for a while and then sold used for thirty pounds. Or perhaps the cloak was worth thirty pounds, not sixty.

Engine continued, "The plush, sir, cost three pounds, ten shillings a yard! And then there is the cost of the lace and velvet."

This was a very fancy and very expensive cloak.

"I shall, Engine, be looked at prettily when I wear it!" Fitzdottrel said. "Are thou sure the play is played today?"

Engine handed Fitzdottrel a paper and said, "Oh, here's the playbill, sir. I forgot to give it to you."

"Ha? *The Devil is an Ass*!" Fitzdottrel said. "I will not lose you, sirrah — I will not miss this play! But, Engine, do you think that the gallant is so furious in his folly? So mad upon the matter that he'll part with his cloak upon these terms you have told me?"

Engine said, "Trust not your Engine —"

Good advice, that.

He continued, "— if the gallant will not part with the cloak upon those terms, then break me to pieces, as you would a rotten crane or an old rusty jack-tool that does not have one true wheel. Do just talk with him."

"I shall do that to satisfy you, Engine," Fitzdottrel said, "and myself, too."

Fitzdottrel went to Wittipol and Manly and said, "With your leave, gentlemen, which of you is he who is so complete an idolater to my wife's beauty, and so very prodigal to my patience, that for the short parley of one swift quarter-hour's conversation with my wife he will part with — let me see — this cloak here, the price of folly?"

Fitzdottrel thought that Wittipol was a fool to part with the cloak in return for fifteen minutes' conversation with Fitzdottrel's wife. Readers may think that Fitzdottrel was a fool for accepting the cloak in return for allowing Wittipol to have fifteen minutes' conversation with Fitzdottrel's wife.

He turned to Wittipol and asked, "Sir, are you the man?"

"I am that venturer, sir," Wittipol said.

"Very good!" Fitzdottrel said. "Your name is Wittipol?"

"Yes, sir."

"And it is told to me that you've travelled lately?"

"That I have, sir."

"Truly, your travels may have altered your complexion," Fitzdottrel said. "But surely, your intelligence stood still."

"It may well be, sir," Wittipol said. "All heads have not the same growth."

Travel can alter people. It can make a complexion darker, and it can broaden one's intelligence. Fitzdottrel was saying that Wittipol's complexion may have changed, but his intelligence had remained the same — he had not grown more intelligent.

"The good man's gravity that left you land, your father, never taught you these pleasant matches?" Fitzdottrel asked.

The word "match" has several meanings: 1) a husband or wife or lover, 2) an opponent, 3) a contest, and 4) a bargain.

Fitzdottrel was asking if Wittipol's late father had taught him to make such bargains as the one Wittipol was now proposing. Perhaps the reason for Wittipol's making such bargains was his father.

"No, nor can his mirth — the mirth of those with whom I make these pleasant matches — put me off," Wittipol said.

Fitzdottrel was smiling at what he thought was the foolishness of Wittipol's making such a bargain.

"You are resolved then to make this bargain?" Fitzdottrel asked.

"Yes, sir."

"Beauty is the saint you'll sacrifice yourself to the very shirt?"

Would Wittipol give up his cloak and strip himself to the shirt in order to talk to a beautiful woman — another man's wife — for fifteen minutes?

"So long as I may still clothe, and keep warm your wisdom!" Wittipol said.

The cloak would clothe Fitzdottrel and keep him warm; in addition, Wittipol would still have clothing to wear.

Wittipol was using the word "wisdom" ironically when using it to refer to Fitzdottrel. Each man thought that the other man was a fool. Currently, both men were right. Wittipol was pursuing Fitzdottrel's wife, and Fitzdottrel was allowing Wittipol access to his wife.

"You lade me, sir!" Fitzdottrel said.

Fitzdottrel meant that Wittipol was lading him with a cloak — Wittipol was putting a cloak on Fitzdottrel's back. One meaning of the verb "to lade" is "to load with gifts." Readers may be forgiven for thinking of an ass being laden with a load.

Yet another meaning of "to lade" was "to burden with guilt." Certainly, Fitzdottrel ought to feel guilty about the way he was acquiring this cloak, expensive as it may be.

"I know what you will bear, sir," Wittipol replied.

An ass can bear a heavy load. Fitzdottrel could bear a heavy load of insults.

"Well, let's get to the point," Fitzdottrel said. "The point of this bargain is only, sir, you say, to speak to my wife?"

"Yes, it is only to speak to her."

"And in my presence?"

"In your very presence."

"And in my hearing?"

"Yes, in your hearing — as long as you do not interrupt us," Wittipol said.

"For the short space you demand, the fourth part of an hour, I think I shall, with some convenient study, and this good help to boot" — Fitzdottrel lifted the cloak — "bring myself to agree to it."

He shrugged himself into the cloak.

"I ask for no more," Wittipol said.

"If you please, walk toward my house," Fitzdottrel said. "Speak what you wish; that time is yours. My right I have departed with. But look for not a minute, or a second, beyond the fifteen minutes I have agreed to. Drawing out the length of time may much advance these matches, and so I will not allow it. And I forbid all kissing. Kisses are silent petitions always with willing lovers."

Fitzdottrel knew that Wittipol wished to seduce his wife.

"Lovers?" Wittipol said. "How does your delusive imagination arrive at that fantasy?"

Wittipol wanted to be her lover — her only lover. Singular.

"Sir, I do know something," Fitzdottrel said. "I forbid all lip-work."

"I am not eager to go at forbidden dainties," Wittipol said. "He who covets unfit things denies himself."

He who covets unfit things denies himself the opportunity to be the best that he can be.

According to most people, Wittipol's pursuing Fitzdottrel's wife was unfit, but Wittipol regarded that wife as very fit, indeed. Wittipol may have convinced himself that pursuing Fitzdottrel's wife was fitting for such a man as himself; he certainly regarded himself with more respect than he regarded Fitzdottrel.

"You say well, sir," Fitzdottrel said. "That was prettily said, that same. He does indeed deny himself.

"I'll have no touches, therefore, nor takings by the arms, nor tender circles cast about the waist — no hugs. Instead, all must be done at a distance.

"Love is brought up with those soft, dainty, delicate handlings. His pulse lies in his palm; and I forbid all melting joints and fingers. That's my bargain I make with you — I forbid anything like physical action and touching.

"But talk, sir, and say whatever you will. Use all the tropes, figures of speech, and rhetorical devices that the classical rhetorician Prince Quintilian can give to you, and much good may it do your rhetoric's heart. You are welcome, sir."

He then said, "Engine, may God be with you."

Wittipol said, "Sir, I must add the condition that I am allowed to have this gentleman — my friend Manly — present as a witness."

"Well, I agree, as long as he is silent," Fitzdottrel said.

"Yes, sir," Manly agreed.

Wittipol, Manly, and Engine exited.

Pug had told Fitzdottrel that his name was "Devil," and so Fitzdottrel called him that.

Fitzdottrel said to Pug, "Come, Devil, I'll make you room in my house very soon. But I'll show you first to your mistress, who's no common one, you must conceive, that brings this gain to see her."

His wife was so beautiful that she had brought an expensive cloak into his possession.

Fitzdottrel said to Pug, "I hope that thou have brought me good luck."

"I shall do that, sir," Pug said.

Wittipol, Manly, and Engine talked together in a room in Fitzdottrel's house.

Wittipol said, "Engine, you hope to get your half piece? There it is, sir."

He gave Engine eleven shillings and said, "Leave now."

Engine took the money and exited.

Wittipol tapped Manly, who was staring into space, on his chest and said, "Friend Manly, who's within here? Are you transfixed?"

"I am entirely in a fit of wonder," Manly said. "What'll be the outcome of this conversation you will have with Fitzdottrel's wife?"

"As for that, don't vex yourself until the outcome reveals itself," Wittipol said. "How do you like Fitzdottrel?"

"I would gladly see more of him," Manly said.

"What do you think about this?" Wittipol asked.

"I am past all degrees and all possible stages of logical thinking," Manly said. "Old Africa and the new America with all their progeny of monsters cannot show so complete a freak as is Fitzdottrel!"

"Could you have believed, without seeing it yourself, that a mind so sordid inward should be so outwardly handsome and laid forth abroad to all the show that ever shop or ware was?" Wittipol asked. "He dresses as if he were a model advertising fine clothing."

Fitzdottrel's mind was sordid: dirty and ignoble. Despite this, however, he presented a handsome outward appearance — thus his appreciation of fine clothing and the expensive cloak that Wittipol had offered to him as a bribe to be allowed to talk to his wife.

"I believe anything now, although I confess that his vices are the most extreme I ever knew in nature," Manly said. "But why does he loves the Devil so much?"

"Oh, sir!" Wittipol said. "He loves the Devil because of the hidden treasure he hopes to find, and he has proposed to himself that there is so infinite a mass of treasure to be recovered that he doesn't care how much he transfers of his present wealth to his men of art — his conjurors — who are the race of men who may coin him: They are the kind of men who can take him and use him to make money for themselves. Make promises of mountains of gold, and the covetous are always the most prodigal."

Conjurors were supposed to be able to get devils to tell them where treasure was hidden. Fitzdottrel believed that he would get mountains of gold, and so he was paying conjurors lots of money in anticipation of his great future wealth.

"But do you have faith that Fitzdottrel will hold to his part of the bargain?" Manly asked.

"Oh, dear sir!" Wittipol said. "He will not fail to live up to his part of the bargain. Fear him not. I know him. One baseness always accompanies another."

Fitzdottrel's accepting the cloak was one baseness; allowing Wittipol to speak to his wife was another.

Wittipol looked up and said, "See! He is here already, and his wife, too."

Manly said about Fitzdottrel's wife, "She is a wondrously beautiful creature — that statement is as true as the statement that I live is true!"

Fitzdottrel said, "Come, wife, this is the gentleman. No, don't blush."

"Why, what do you mean, sir?" Mrs. Frances Fitzdottrel said. "Do you still have your reason? Or have you lost your mind?"

"Wife, I don't know that I have lent it forth to anyone, at least, without a pawn, wife, or that I've eaten or drunk the thing lately that should corrupt it," Fitzdottrel said. "Therefore, gentle wife, obey me. It is thy virtue. Don't argue with me."

In this society, a good wife was an obedient wife.

"Aren't you already enough the talk of feasts and meetings?" Mrs. Frances Fitzdottrel asked. "Must you make a new topic for fresh gossip?"

Fitzdottrel said, "Why, careful wedlock — that is, you, my worried wife — if I have a longing to have one more tale told about me, what is that to thee, dear heart? Why should thou resent my delight, or cross it, by being solicitous when it doesn't concern thee?"

"This does concern me," Mrs. Frances Fitzdottrel said. "Yes, I have a share in this. The scorn will fall as bitterly on me, where both you and me are laughed at."

"Laughed at, sweet bird?" Fitzdottrel said. "Is that what you have scruples about? Come, come, thou are a nyas."

A nyas is an unfledged bird. An eyas is an unfledged hawk taken out of the nest for training. These words, however, were sometimes used interchangeably. Young birds are innocent, and when they are taken out of the nest, they cry. Fitzdottrel was saying that his wife was naïve.

Fitzdottrel continued, "Which of your great houses — I will not mean at home, here, but abroad — your families in France, wife, do not send forth something within a seven-years'-time that may be laughed at? I do not say seven months, nor seven weeks, nor seven days, nor seven hours, but seven years, wife. I give them time. Once, within seven years, I think they may do something that may be laughed at, in France — I keep my opinion about this, still."

His point was that people in great houses — higher-class people — were laughed at; therefore, he was in good company. He was patriotic, however, and so talked about families in France.

He continued, "Therefore, wife, let them who wish to always laugh at me rather than weep for me.

"Here is a cloak that cost fifty pounds, wife, which I can sell for thirty, after I have seen all London in it, and London has seen me in it."

Engine had said that the cloak was never made for under sixty pounds, but Fitzdottrel was a good judge of clothing and knew its worth.

He continued, "Today, I go to the Blackfriars Playhouse to see *The Devil is an Ass*. I will sit where people can see me, salute all my acquaintance, rise up between the acts, let fall my cloak, show everyone that I am a handsome man and that I have an expensive suit of clothing — that's the special reason why we go to the theater: to be seen. That is true of all of us who pretend to stand to show displeasure for what is on the stage."

If a man disliked a certain playwright, that man could attend one of the playwright's shows, and in between acts stand up with an expression of disgust and ostentatiously leave — it did not matter whether the play was good or bad. Of course, a person could also do that as a way of being the center of attention and displaying his fine clothing.

Fitzdottrel continued, "The ladies ask, who's that? For they come to see us, love, as we come to see them. Shall I lose all this because of the false fear of being laughed at?"

He said sarcastically, "Yes, certainly!"

He then continued without sarcasm, "Let them laugh, wife. Let me have such another cloak tomorrow, and let them laugh again, wife, and again, and then grow fat with laughing, and then fatter, all my young gallants — and let them bring their friends, too, to laugh at me.

"Shall I forbid them? No, let heaven forbid them. Or let their intelligence forbid them, if intelligence has any kind of control of them."

Fitzdottrel took her to the side and spoke privately to her: "Come, give me thy ear, wife. That is all I'll borrow of thee."

He said to Wittipol, "Set your watch, sir."

He said privately to his wife, "Thou are to only listen, and not speak a word, dove, to anything he says. I tell you that in precept, and as an order. This is no less than counsel, on your wifehood, wife. Do not speak to him even if he flatters you, or courts you, or flirts with you, as you must expect him to do, or let's say, if he rails at you — whatever his skills are, wife, I will have thee delude them with a trick, which is thy obstinate silence.

"I know advantages, and I love to hit these meddling young men at their own weapons. He will use eloquence, and your response of silence will neutralize him."

Fitzdottrel led his wife to a place for her to stand, and he set his watch.

He then said to Wittipol, "Is your watch ready? Here my sail bears, for you."

He said to his wife, "Tack toward him, sweet pinnace."

Women were often figuratively called pinnaces, which were small sailing boats; however, other meanings of "pinnace" included "prostitute" and the sexual meaning of "mistress."

In a way, Fitzdottrel was prostituting his wife for a cloak.

Fitzdottrel asked Wittipol, "Where's your watch?"

Wittipol answered, "I'll set it, sir, with yours."

They were synchronizing their watches so they could agree when fifteen minutes had ended.

Mrs. Frances Fitzdottrel said to herself, "I must obey my husband."

Noticing how sad she looked, Manly thought, *Her modesty seems to suffer with her beauty, and so, as if his folly were away, it were worth pity.*

He meant this: Because her modesty seemed to suffer with her beauty, she was worthy of pity. And if Fitzdottrel were not capable of such folly, he would be worthy of pity.

Or, possibly, he meant this: Because her modesty seemed to suffer with her beauty, then if Fitzdottrel were not capable of such folly, her modesty and her beauty — that is, she herself — would be worthy of pity. If this is what he meant, he was blaming her for marrying a fool.

Or, possibly, he meant this: Because her modesty seemed to suffer with her beauty, then if Fitzdottrel were not capable of such folly and therefore was not deserving of punishment by being made an ass of, it would be good to pity her and not continue with this situation.

Fitzdottrel compared his watch with Wittipol's watch and said, "Now thou are right; begin, sir. But first, let me repeat the contract briefly.

"I am, sir, to freely enjoy this cloak I am wearing, as your gift, upon the condition that you may as freely speak here to my spouse your quarter of an hour, always keeping the measured distance of your yard, or more, away from my said spouse, and in my sight and hearing."

In this society, one meaning of "yard" was "penis."

He then asked Wittipol, "This is your covenant — your agreement — with me?

"Yes, but you'll allow for this time we spent just now?" Wittipol asked.

Fitzdottrel had spent a few seconds going over their covenant.

"Let's set our watches back that much time," Fitzdottrel said.

Changing his mind, Wittipol said, "I think I shall not need the extra time."

"Well, begin, sir," Fitzdottrel said. "There is your boundary, sir. Do not go beyond that rush-mat."

"If you interrupt me, sir, I shall discloak you," Wittipol said.

He then began speaking to Mrs. Frances Fitzdottrel:

"The time I have purchased, lady, is but short, and therefore, if I employ it thriftily, I hope I stand the nearer to my pardon. I am not here to tell you that you are fair, or lovely, or how well you dress yourself, lady; I'll save myself that eloquence of your mirror, which can speak these things better to you than I. And it is a knowledge wherein fools may be as wise as a court parliament."

During medieval times, a court of ladies would rule on questions of courtly love.

Wittipol continued, "Nor do I come with any prejudice — preconceived idea — or doubt that you should, to the realization of your own worth, need least revelation. She's a simple woman who does not know her good — whoever knows her ill — and in every respect."

A proverb stated, "Any woman is simple-minded who fails to know what's best for her."

Wittipol continued, "That you are the wife to so much blighted flesh as scarcely has soul, instead of salt, to keep it sweet, I think will need no witnesses to prove."

The soul keeps the body alive and preserves it from rotting, just as salt preserves the flesh of animals for eating. Fitzdottrel's covetousness showed that he had little soul.

Wittipol continued, "The cold sheets that you lie in, with the watching candle that sees how, dull to any thaw of beauty, bits and pieces of time, and quarter nights, half nights, and whole nights, sometimes, the devil-given elfin

— malignant — squire your husband leaves you, quitting here his proper circle for a much worse one in the walks of Lincoln's Inn, under the elms, to expect the fiend in vain there, will confess for you. All of these things are evidence of how your husband regards you."

Wittipol was pointing out that Fitzdottrel neglected her: his wife. He left her circle — her vagina — in order to go to the walks of Lincoln's Inn to see a conjuror's circle in the vain hope of seeing the Devil.

"I looked for this nonsense," Fitzdottrel said. "I expected you to say such things."

Wittipol continued, "And what a daughter of darkness he makes you, locked up away from all society you wish to visit or object you wish to see.

"Your eye is not allowed to look upon a face under a conjurer's — or under some mold, aka top of a head, hollow and lean like his — except but by such great means as I now make to allow you to see my face."

Wittipol meant that Mrs. Frances Fitzdottrel was allowed to look at no male faces except those under a conjuror's mold or crown (both words mean "top of head") or the face that was under her husband's mold or crown, which was hollow (due to lacking a brain) and lean (the human brain is mostly made of fat: almost 60 percent).

He continued, "Your own too acutely felt sufferings, without the extraordinary aids of spells or spirits, may assure you, lady."

Assure her of what? Wittipol was hoping that her acutely felt sufferings would assure her that she ought to spend time with him.

"As for my part, I protest against all such practice. I work by no false arts, medicines, or charms to be said forward and backward."

Fitzdottrel said, "No, I object —"

"Sir, I shall ease you of the burden of that cloak," Wittipol said.

He made a motion as if he were going to take the cloak from him.

Fitzdottrel said, "I am mum."

Wittipol said to Mrs. Frances Fitzdottrel, "Nor have I designs, lady, upon you more than this: to tell you how Love, Beauty's good angel, he who waits upon her at all occasions, and no less than Fortune helps the adventurous, in me makes that proffer which never fair one was so fond to lose who could but reach a hand forth to her freedom.

"On the first sight I loved you; since which time, though I have travelled, I have been in travail more for this second blessing of your eyes that now I've purchased than for all aims else.

"Think about it, lady. Let your mind be as active as is your beauty; view your object well. Examine both my fashion and my years.

"Things that are like are soon familiar; and Nature joys still in equality."

Wittipol was referring to two proverbs: "Like will to like" and "Marry your equal." He did not think that Fitzdottrel was Mrs. Frances Fitzdottrel's equal, and he did think that he himself and Mrs. Frances Fitzdottrel were alike.

He continued, "Let not the sign of the husband frighten you, lady, but before your spring is gone, enjoy it. Flowers, though fair, are often but of one morning. Think, all beauty does not last until the autumn."

He was referring to this proverb: "Beauty does fade like a flower." And, of course, he was advising her to seize the day: *Carpe diem.*

Wittipol continued, "You grow old while I tell you this. And such as cannot use the present are not wise. If Love and Fortune will take care of us, why should our will be wanting? This is all. What do you answer, lady?"

Mrs. Frances Fitzdottrel stood mute.

Her husband thought, *Now the entertainment comes. Let him continue to wait, wait, wait, while the watch goes, and the time runs.*

Mrs. Frances Fitzdottrel made a motion as if she would speak, and her husband thought, *Wife!* He shook his head at her.

"What!" Wittipol said. "You don't speak any word? No, and so then I taste a trick in it. Worthy lady, I cannot be so false to my own thoughts of your presumed goodness to conceive this as your rudeness, which I see is imposed. Yet since your cautelous — crafty, wily — jailer here stands by you, and you're denied the liberty of the house, let me take warrant, lady, from your silence — which always is interpreted as consent — to make your answer for you, which shall be to as good purpose as I can imagine, and what I think you'd speak."

Since Mrs. Frances Fitzdottrel would not speak, he would speak in her behalf.

He moved Manly, his friend, in front of him.

Fitzdottrel objected, "No, no, no, no!"

Manly was beyond the rush-mat and close to Mrs. Frances Fitzdottrel.

"I shall resume, sir," Wittipol said to Fitzdottrel.

He moved Manly back behind the rush-mat.

"Sir, what do you mean?" Manly asked Wittipol. "What are you doing?"

Wittipol said to Fitzdottrel, "One interruption more, sir, and you go into your hose and doublet, and nothing saves you. You will get no cloak."

Because Manley was now behind the rush-mat and at least a yard's distance from Fitzdottrel's wife, Fitzdottrel ought not to object.

Wittipol then said to Fitzdottrel, "And therefore listen. This is for your wife."

Manly would represent Wittipol, and Wittipol would represent Mrs. Frances Fitzdottrel and speak for her: He was going to speak the words that he wished she would say to him.

Not quite sure what was going on, Manly said to Wittipol, "You must play fair, sir."

Wittipol said to Manly, "Stand for me, good friend. Represent me as I represent Mrs. Frances Fitzdottrel and speak for her."

Wittipol then pretended to be Mrs. Frances Fitzdottrel and spoke the words that he wished that she would say to him:

"Truly, sir, what you have uttered about my unequal and so sordid match here, with all the circumstances of my bondage, is more than true.

"I have a husband, and a two-legged one, but he is such a moonling — a lunatic and an idiot — as no wit of man or roses can redeem from being an ass."

In the *Metamorphoses* of Apuleius, a work that is sometimes called *The Golden Ass*, a man named Lucius is transformed into an ass. He recovers his human form by eating roses.

Wittipol continued speaking the words that he wished Mrs. Frances Fitzdottrel would say to him:

"He's grown too much the story told by men's mouths to escape his lading, aka burden. Should I make it my study, and plan all ways, and indeed even call mankind to help to take his burden off — why, this one act of his, to let his wife out to be courted, and at a price, proclaims his asinine nature so loudly as I am weary of my title — my legal right as his wife — to him.

"But sir, you seem a gentleman of virtue no less than of good birth, and one who in every way looks as he were of too good quality to entrap a credulous woman, or betray her.

"Since you have paid thus dearly, sir, for a visit, and made such venture on your wit and charge — the cloak — merely to see me, or at most to speak to me, I would be too stupid, or — what's worse — too much of an ingrate if I were not to return your venture.

"Think but how I may with safety do it; I shall trust my love and honor to you, and I shall presume you'll always husband and protect both my love and honor against this husband — who, if we chance to change his liberal ears to other ensigns, and with labor make a new beast of him, as he shall deserve, cannot complain he is unkindly dealt with."

By committing adultery with Wittipol, she would change her husband's ass' ears to the horns of a cuckold. (Men with unfaithful wives were said to have invisible horns growing out of their forehead.)

Wittipol continued speaking the words he wished Mrs. Frances Fitzdottrel would say to him:

"This day he is to go to a new play, sir, from whence no fear, no, nor authority, scarcely the King's command, sir, will restrain him, now that you have fitted him with a garment he can wear while sitting on the stage, for the mere name's sake, were there nothing else."

The name of the play was *The Devil is an Ass*. Fitzdottrel would certainly want to see a play about devils; in addition, Wittipol had made an ass of the "devil" named Fitzdottrel by successfully tempting him with a cloak.

Wittipol continued speaking the words he wished Mrs. Frances Fitzdottrel would say to him:

"And many more such journeys he will make, which, if they now or any time hereafter offer us opportunity, you hear, sir, me who'll be as glad and eager to embrace, meet, and enjoy it as cheerfully as you."

Wittipol now resumed his own voice and moved beside Manly and said to Mrs. Frances Fitzdottrel, "I humbly thank you, lady."

"Keep your ground, sir," Fitzdottrel said.

He did not need to say that. Wittipol was still a yard away from Fitzdottrel's wife.

"Will you be lightened by the removal of a cloak?" Wittipol said to Fitzdottrel.

Fitzdottrel said, "I am mum."

Wittipol said to Mrs. Frances Fitzdottrel, "And except that I am, by the solemn contract, thus to take my leave of you at this so envious distance, I would have taught our lips before this to seal the happy mixture made of our souls. But we must both now yield to the necessity of our parting.

"Yet do not doubt, lady, that I can kiss, and touch, and laugh, and whisper, and do those crowning courtships, too, for which day and the public have allowed no name — but now my bargain binds me and I must leave.

"It would be a rude injury to importune you any more, or urge a noble nature to what of its own bounty it already is prone to; otherwise, I would speak. But, lady, I love so well as I will hope you'll do so, too."

Wittipol then said to Fitzdottrel, "I have finished, sir."

"Well, then, have I won?" Fitzdottrel asked.

Had he won the cloak? And had he won the contest for his wife?

"Sir," Wittipol said, "and I may win, too."

Fitzdottrel had won the cloak, but Wittipol hoped to win the wife.

Fitzdottrel said, sarcastically, "Oh, yes! No doubt of it. I'll take care to order that my wife shall hang forth signs at the window to tell you when I am absent. Or I'll keep three or four footmen ready always whose job shall be to run and fetch you when my wife longs to see you, sir. I'll go and order a gilt luxurious coach for her and you to take the air in — yes, you two shall ride into Hyde Park and thence into Blackfriars so you can visit the painters, where you may see pictures, and note the most good-looking limbs, and how to make them."

The paintings would be of lovers. Wittipol and Fitzdottrel's wife could study the paintings so that they could imitate the positions of the lovers.

Fitzdottrel continued, "Or what do you say to a middling gossip — a female go-between or panderer — to bring you together at her lodging under pretext of teaching my wife some rare recipe for making almond milk? Ha? It shall be a part of my care for my wife.

"Good sir, may God be with you. I have kept the contract, and the cloak is mine."

"Why, much good may it do you, sir," Wittipol said. "It may turn out that you have bought it at a high price, although I have not sold it."

"A pretty riddle!" Fitzdottrel said. "Fare you well, good sir."

Fitzdottrel turned his wife around so that she was not facing Wittipol as he said to her, "Wife, turn your face this way."

He then said, "Look at me, and think you've had a wicked dream, wife, and forget it."

Manly said, "This is the strangest puppet show I ever saw."

He had witnessed a strange performance.

Wittipol and Manly exited.

Fitzdottrel said, "Now, wife, does this fair cloak sit the worse upon me for my great sufferings, or your little patience? Does it? Do they laugh, do you think?"

His wife replied, "Why, sir, and you might see them laughing. What they think about you may be soon known by paying attention to the words of the young gentleman's speech."

"Young gentleman?" Fitzdottrel said. "By God's death! You are in love with him, are you? Couldn't he be called 'the gentleman,' without the 'young'? Go up to your room again."

"My cage, you were best to call it!" she replied.

"Yes, sing there," Fitzdottrel said. "You'd prefer to be making blanc-manger with him at your mother's! I know you."

Blanc-manger is a dish made mainly of white ingredients, including fowl. Semen is white or whitish-gray, and Fitzdottrel was saying that his wife would prefer to be creating semen with Wittipol. In this society, the word "fowl" often meant "whore."

He ordered his wife, "Go get you up to your room."

His wife exited.

Pug the devil entered the room.

Fitzdottrel said, "How are you now! What do you say, Devil?"

"Here is a man named Engine, sir, who desires to speak with you," Pug said.

"I thought he would bring some news about a broker!" Fitzdottrel said. "Well, let him come in, good Devil — or fetch him."

Pug exited, and Engine entered the room.

Fitzdottrel said, "Oh, my fine Engine! What's the affair? More cheaters?"

"No sir," Engine said. "The wit, the brain, the great projector I told you of, has newly come to town."

"Where is he, Engine?"

"I have brought him with me — he's outside," Engine said. "I brought him here even before he had time to pull off his boots, sir, but even so he was followed by people interested in conducting business with him."

"You say that he is a projector, but what is a projector?" Fitzdottrel said. "I would like to understand that."

Engine answered, "Why, a projector is a man, sir, who projects ways to enrich men, or to make them great, by petitions, by marriages, by undertakings, according as he sees they fancy it."

People could petition the King for a monopoly to make a product or perform a service.

"Can't he at all conjure?" Fitzdottrel said.

"I think he can, sir — to tell you the truth — but you know that recently the government has taken such note of conjurors, and compelled them to enter such great bonds, that the conjurors dare not practice their art," Engine said.

"That is true," Fitzdottrel said, "and I lie fallow for it all the while!"

In 1615, King James I had ordered the Lord Mayor of London to enforce more rigorously the laws restraining conjurors.

"Oh, sir!" Engine said. "You'll grow the richer for the rest — the lying fallow — you are taking now."

"I hope I shall," Fitzdottrel said. "But Engine, you talk somewhat too much about my courses of action. My cloak-customer could tell me strange particulars."

The cloak-customer — Wittipol — knew about Fitzdottrel's dealings with conjurors, and Fitzdottrel believed that Engine must have told him about those dealings.

"By my means?" Engine asked.

"How else could he know about my courses of action?" Fitzdottrel said.

"You do not know, sir, what he has, and by what arts," Engine said. "He is a moneyed man, sir, and he is as greatly involved with your almanac-men as you are!"

"Almanac-men" were men who created almanacs that contained weather predictions and medical lore. They were often astrologers.

"That gallant?" Fitzdottrel asked.

Uncomfortable, Engine changed the subject.

"You make the other man wait too long here," Engine said, "and he is extremely punctual."

"Is he a gallant?" Fitzdottrel asked.

"Sir, you shall see," Engine said. "He's in his riding suit, as he comes now from Court. But hear him speak. Minister matter to him, and then tell me whether he is a gallant."

CHAPTER 2

— 2.1 —

Merecraft the projector, Trains (Merecraft's manservant), and three waiters entered the room, joining Fitzdottrel and Engine. The waiters were possibly the attendants of Merecraft's clients and were waiting to get instructions from Merecraft. Or possibly they were helping Merecraft to con Fitzdottrel.

Merecraft was accurately named. His name meant "only tricks": He was a con man who preyed on the greed of his clients. By promising to make them rich, he was able to get their money for himself.

He said to Fitzdottrel, "Sir, money's a whore, a bawd, a drudge, fit to run out on errands; let her go. *Via, pecunia!*"

This was Latin for "The way or path, the money!" The Italian *via*, however, meant "away" or "leave" or "onward."

Merecraft wanted Fitzdottrel to let his money go so he — Merecraft — could possess it.

He continued, "When she's run and gone, and fled and dead, then I will fetch her again with aqua-vitae — distilled spirits — out of an old barrel. While there are lees of wine, or dregs of beer, I'll never lack money."

He would use the lees of wine or dregs of beer to distill aqua-vitae.

He continued, "Coin her out of cobwebs and dust, but I'll have her! Raise wool upon eggshells, sir, and make grass grow out of marrow-bones to make her come."

Merecraft said to the first waiter, "Commend me to your mistress. Tell her, let the thousand pounds just be had ready, and it is done."

The first waiter exited.

Merecraft said, "I would just like to see the creature of flesh and blood, the man, the prince, indeed, who could employ so many millions as I would help him to."

Fitzdottrel said to Engine, "How he talks! Millions?"

Merecraft said to the second waiter, "I'll give you an account of this tomorrow."

The second waiter exited.

Merecraft said, "Yes, I will talk no less, and do it, too, if they were myriads — and without the devil, by direct means; it shall be good in law."

He was talking about making millions without the help of conjuring. He was claiming to be able to do so legally.

King James I of England opposed conjuring.

"Sir," Engine said.

Merecraft said to the third waiter, "Tell Master Woodcock I'll not fail to meet him upon the Exchange at night. Tell him to have the documents there, and we'll dispatch the business."

A woodcock is a proverbially stupid bird.

The third waiter exited.

Merecraft turned to Fitzdottrel and said, "Sir, you are a gentleman of a good presence, a handsome man. I have considered you as a fit stock to graft honors upon. I have a project to make you a duke now.

"That you must be one, within so many months as I set down out of true reason of state, you shall not avoid it. But you must listen, then."

"Listen?" Engine said. "Why, sir, do you doubt his ears? Alas! You do not know Master Fitzdottrel."

"Do you doubt his ears?" meant 1) "Do you think he is deaf?" and 2) "Do you doubt that he has the ears of an ass?"

"He does not know me indeed," Fitzdottrel said. "I thank you, Engine, for rectifying and correcting him."

"Good!" Merecraft said.

He turned to Engine and said, "Why, Engine, then I'll tell it to you — I see you have credit here, and I'll not question that you can keep counsel. He shall be only an undertaker — a business partner — with me in a most feasible business. It shall cost him nothing —"

"Good, sir," Engine said.

"— unless he wants to invest money," Merecraft said. "But he shall lend his countenance — that I will have — to appear in it to great men, for which I'll make him one."

Fitzdottrel would join with him in business, and that support would help impress great men — according to Merecraft. In return for Fitzdottrel's support, Merecraft would make Fitzdottrel a great man — or so Merecraft said he would do.

Men can be greedy for social status just as they can be greedy for money.

Merecraft continued, "He shall not open his wallet. I'll drive his patent — execute his commission, his royal license — for him."

King James I of England gave monopolies to people to perform certain tasks that would result in profit for them and for the Crown.

Merecraft continued, "We'll take in — include — citizens, commoners, and aldermen to bear the expenses, and blow them off again like so many dead flies when the business is carried."

He was saying that he and Fitzdottrel would work with other people. The other people would pay the expenses. Sharing the profits was another matter. ("Take in" also means "deceive.")

Red flag, that.

Merecraft continued, "The thing is for recovery of drowned land, whereof the Crown will have its moiety if it be owner; else, the Crown and landowners will share that moiety, and the recoverers of the drowned land will enjoy the other moiety for their return on their investment."

Draining a swamp recovered land that could be used for profitable purposes.

A moiety is a share or part.

"The recovery of drowned land will take place throughout England?" Engine asked.

"Yes, which will arise to eighteen millions, seven the first year," Merecraft said. "I have computed all, and made my survey down to the last acre. I'll begin at the hollow, the lowest ground, not at the outskirts, the edges — as some have done, and lost all that they wrought, their timber-work, their trench, their banks all borne away, or else filled up with water again by the next winter. Tut, they never went the right and best way; I'll have it all."

"A gallant tract of land it is!" Engine said.

"It will yield a pound an acre," Merecraft said. "We must rent cheap, always, at first."

He then said to Fitzdottrel, "But sir, this project looks too large for you, I see. Come hither, we'll have a lesser project."

He motioned to Trains, his manservant, and said, "Here's a plain fellow, you see him. He has his papers there, in a black buckram bag, and it will not be sold for the Earldom of Pancridge."

No Earldom of Pancridge exists.

Merecraft then said to Trains, "Draw one out at random, and give it to me."

Trains drew a paper out of the bag and gave it to him.

Merecraft said, "Project four. Dog skins? Twelve thousand pounds! The very worst, drawn out at first."

Twelve thousand pounds is a lot of money, but according to Merecraft, this was the worst and least profitable of his moneymaking ideas.

"Please, let's see it, sir," Fitzdottrel said.

"It is a toy, a trifle!" Merecraft said.

"A trifle!" Fitzdottrel said. "Twelve thousand pounds for dogs' skins?"

"Yes," Merecraft said, "but you must know, sir, by my way of preparing and treating the leather to a height of better-quality goods, like your borachio of Spain, sir —"

A Spanish borachio is a wine bottle made from pigskin or goatskin.

Merecraft continued, "— I can fetch nine thousand for it —"

"From the King's glover?" Engine asked.

Engine, another con man, was making it sound as if King James I of England was interested in purchasing great numbers of dog-skin gloves.

"Yes," Merecraft said, "how did you hear that?"

"Sir, I know you can," Engine said.

"Within this hour I can, and reserve half my secret," Merecraft said.

He said to Engine, "Pluck another paper. See if thou have a more fortunate hand than Trains."

Engine plucked out a second paper: one marked "Bottle-ale."

Merecraft said, "I thought so. The very next worse to it! Bottle-ale. Yet, this is two-and-twenty thousand! Please pull out another two or three papers."

"Good man," Fitzdottrel said. "Wait, friend, by bottle-ale, you can make twenty-two thousand pounds?"

"Yes, sir," Merecraft said. "It's calculated to a penny-halfpenny-farthing. On the back of the paper, you may see it there. Read it.

"I will not reduce a harrington of the sum."

A harrington is a farthing; it was named for Lord Harrington, who had a patent from the King that allowed him to coin farthings.

Merecraft continued, "I'll win the sum in my water for making ale, and my malt, my furnaces, and the hanging of my copper vessels, the barreling, and the subtlety of my yeast, and then the earth — the clay — of my bottles, which I dig, turn up, and steep, and work, and fire in a kiln myself to a degree of porcelain.

"You will wonder at my calculations of what I will put up in seven years! For so long a time I ask for my invention."

It would take seven years to produce and age the ale.

Merecraft continued, "I will save in cork, in my mere stoppering of the bottles, above three thousand pounds within that period of time, by gouging out the stoppers just to the size of my bottles, and not slicing the cork. There's infinite loss in slicing the cork."

Engine drew out another paper, which was marked "Raisins."

"What have thou there?" Merecraft asked. "Oh, making wine out of raisins; this is in hand, now."

Engine asked, "Isn't it strange, sir, to make wine out of raisins?"

"Yes," Merecraft said, "and as true a wine as the wines of France, or Spain, or Italy. Look at what kind of grape my raisin is, that wine I'll render perfectly. From the muscatel grape, I'll render muscatel wine. From the canary grape, I'll render canary wine. From the claret grape, I'll render claret wine. This is true of all kinds of grape, and I'll lessen the prices of wine throughout the kingdom by fifty percent."

"But, sir, what if you raze — wipe out — the other commodity: raisins?" Engine asked.

He was making a joke: punning on "raze" and "raisin."

"Why, then I'll make it out of blackberries, and it shall do the same," Merecraft said. "It will just take more skill, and the expense will be less.

"Take out another paper."

Fitzdottrel said, "No, good sir. Save yourself the trouble. I'll neither look nor hear about any project but your first, there — the drowned land — if it will do as you say."

Merecraft said, "Sir, there's no place to give you demonstration of these things. They are a little too subtle."

Red flag, that.

He continued, "But I could show you that the recovery of drowned land is so necessary that you must end up being what you want to be: a duke.

"You will become a duke despite the popular misconception that England bears no dukes."

For many years in England there were no dukes, but with the accession of King James I, dukes had again appeared in England.

Merecraft said to Fitzdottrel, "If you will keep the land, sir; the greatness of the estate shall throw a dukedom upon you.

"But if you prefer to turn the estate to money instead of keeping the land, what may not you, sir, purchase with that wealth? Say you should part with two of your millions, to be the thing you would be — a duke — who would not do it?

"I say that I myself will, out of my dividend, bid for some pretty principality in Italy, outside the jurisdiction of the church.

"Now you, perhaps, fancy the mists of England rather? But — do you have a private room, sir, for us to withdraw to, to talk in more detail about this project?"

"Oh, yes," Fitzdottrel said.

He called, "Devil!"

Merecraft said, "These, sir, are businesses that need to be carried out with caution, and in a cloud of secrecy."

Red flag, that.

"I apprehend that they need to be done so, sir," Fitzdottrel replied.

Pug entered the room, and Fitzdottrel asked, "Devil, where is your mistress?"

"She is above, sir, in her chamber," Pug replied.

"Oh, that's well," Fitzdottrel said.

He then said to Merecraft, "Then go this way, good sir."

"I shall follow you," Merecraft said.

He then said, "Trains, give me the bag, and go immediately to commend my service to my Lady Tailbush. Tell her I have come from court this morning; say that I've got our business moved, and well. Entreat her to give you the fourscore angels — eighty coins — and see that they are disposed of to my counsel, the lawyer Sir Paul Eitherside. Sometime today I'll wait upon her Ladyship and give her my report."

Trains exited quickly.

Engine said, "Sir, how quickly Trains acts. Do you see?"

Merecraft asked, "Engine, when did you see my cousin Everill? Does he still stay at your quarter in the Bermudas?'

The Bermudas were a bad part of London.

"Yes, sir," Engine said. "He was writing this morning very intensely."

"Don't let him know that I have come to town," Merecraft said. "I have arranged some business for him, but I would take the business to him before he has time to think about it."

Red flag, that.

"Is it past?" Engine asked.

"Not yet," Merecraft said. "It is well on the way."

"Oh, sir!" Engine said. "Your Worship takes infinite pains."

"I love friends to be active," Merecraft said. "A sluggish nature puts off man and woman."

"And such a blessing follows it," Engine said.

"I thank my fate," Merecraft said.

He then said to Fitzdottrel, "Please, let's go somewhere private, sir —"

"In here," Fitzdottrel said.

"— where none may interrupt us," Merecraft said.

He and Engine went into the private room.

Fitzdottrel said to Pug, "Listen, Devil. Lock the street doors fast, and let no one in — unless they are this gentleman's followers — to trouble me.

"Have you been paying attention? You've heard and seen something today, and by it you may gather that my wife is a fruit that's worth the stealing, and therefore she is worth the watching.

"Be sure, now, that you've all your eyes about you; and let in no lace-woman, nor bawd who brings French masks and cut-work embroidery.

"Do you understand? Let in no old crones who sell wafers and convey letters. Let in no youths disguised like country wives with cream and marrow-puddings. Much knavery may be conveyed in a pudding, much bawdy intelligence; they're shrewd ciphers.

"Do not turn the key to any neighbor's need, whether it be only to kindle fire, or beg a little fire — put the fire out, instead. Put it all out, to ashes, so that they may see no smoke.

"Or if neighbors need water, spill it; knock on the empty tubs, so that by the sound the neighbors may be forbidden entry.

"Say that we have been robbed if anyone comes to borrow a spoon, or something else.

"I will not have 'good fortune' or 'God's blessing' let in while I am busy."

Beggars would say, "Good fortune" or "God's blessing," while begging.

Pug said, "I'll take care of it, sir. They shall not trouble you, even if they want to."

"Well, do what I tell you to do," Fitzdottrel said.

He joined Merecraft and Engine in the private room.

Pug said, "I have no singular service of this now, nor no superlative master!"

Pug had come to London to do villainy, but there was nothing singular about that because Londoners were already doing lots of villainy. Also, his master was not superlative. Pug's chief, Satan, wished to do evil, but Pug's earthly master, Fitzdottrel, was doing lots of evil. But Fitzdottrel was not a superlative master because so many people were willing and certainly seemed capable of doing evil to him.

Pug continued, "I shall wish to be in Hell again, and at my leisure!"

And why should he not be at leisure in Hell? People such as Fitzdottrel and Merecraft were already doing lots of evil. Even such a man as Wittipol was devoting himself to tempting a married woman to commit adultery.

Pug continued, "Should I bring a Vice from Hell? That would be as crafty a scheme as to bring broadcloth here to England, or to transport fresh oranges into Spain."

There was no need to transport fresh oranges into Spain because Spain had lots of fresh oranges. There was no need to bring broadcloth here to England because England had lots of broadcloth. There was no need to bring a Vice from Hell to London because London had lots of vice.

He continued, "I find out the truth now. My chief was in the right. Can any fiend boast of a better Vice than by nature and practice they're already owners of here?

"May Hell never own me if I am not impressed by such villainy as is here in London! The fine appeal of it pulls me along! To hear men grown such experts in our subtlest sciences!"

Certainly Merecraft was an expert in the art of conning greedy men.

Pug then said, "My first act now shall be to make this master of mine a cuckold. I will practice the earliest work of darkness!

"I will deserve so well of my fair mistress, by my revelations and useful information first, my advisory counsels afterward, and keeping secret counsel after that, as whosoever is one who sleeps with her, I'll be another; to be sure, I'll have my share. Most delicate damned flesh she will be!"

Pug intended to be one of those who slept with Mrs. Frances Fitzdottrel and cuckolded her husband.

He continued, "Oh, that I could delay time now! Midnight will come too fast upon me, I fear, to cut my pleasure —"

At midnight he would return to Hell, thus cutting the amount of time he would have to sleep with Mrs. Frances Fitzdottrel. Indeed, if midnight came fast enough, he would have no time to sleep with Mrs. Frances Fitzdottrel.

Mrs. Frances Fitzdottrel entered the room and said, "Go to the back door. Someone is knocking; see who it is."

Pug said to himself as he exited, "Dainty she-devil!"

Alone, Mrs. Frances Fitzdottrel said to herself, "I cannot get this venture of the cloak out of my fancy, nor the gentlemanly way Wittipol took, which, though it was strange, yet it was handsome, and had a grace that was beyond the originality.

'Surely he will think me that dull stupid creature he talked about, and may end his attempt to seduce me, if I don't find a way to thank him. He did presume, knowing that I was thinking about it, that I would give him an answer; and he will swear that my brain is very barren if it can yield him no return."

Pug returned.

Mrs. Frances Fitzdottrel asked him, "Who is it at the back door?"

Pug said, "Mistress, it is — but first, let me assure the very best of mistresses that I am, although my master's manservant, my mistress' slave, the servant of her secrets and sweet actions, and I know what fitly will conduce to either."

"What's this? I tell you to come to yourself and think what your job is: to make an answer to my question. Tell me this: Who is it at the door?"

"The gentleman, mistress, who paid the price of a cloak to speak with you this morning, and who expects only to take some small commandments from you — whatever commandments you please that are worthy your form, he says, and your gentlest manners."

"Oh!" she said. "You'll soon prove to be his hired man, I fear. What has he given you for this message?

"Sir, tell him to put off his hopes of straw and stop spreading his nets in full view like this."

"Hopes of straw" are "no hopes." The purpose of the net was to capture her the way that a woodsman would capture a bird.

She continued, "Although the nets may capture Master Fitzdottrel, I am no such fowl — nor a fair one, tell him — who will be had with stalking.

"And tell him to not appear to me at the gentleman's chamber-window in Lincoln's Inn there, that opens to my gallery."

The Fitzdottrels lived next to Lincoln's Inn. Mrs. Frances Fitzdottrel's gallery — a large reception room — was close to a window at Lincoln's Inn.

She continued, "If he does not, I swear that I will acquaint my husband with his folly and leave him to the just rage of his offended jealousy. Or if your master's sense will be not so quick to right me, tell him I shall find a friend who will repair — mend — me. Say I will be quiet in my own house! I tell you, in those words give my message to him."

Her words could be interpreted as a coded message to Wittipol, telling him to 1) communicate with her by making use of the window at Lincoln's Inn, 2) be her "friend" — a word that can mean "lover" — who would mend her, perhaps in bed, and 3) know that she will be quiet in her own house — for example, when her husband was gone.

But her words were deliberately misleading and ambiguous in order to fool Pug: She wanted Pug to think that she was telling Wittipol that he should *not* appear at the window in Lincoln's Inn. The word "friend" did not have to mean "lover." The word "quiet" could mean "unmolested."

Pug said to himself, "This is some fool turned!"

"Turned" meant "out of his — or was it her — wits."

Perhaps he meant, "Wittipol is a fool whom my mistress is turning away."

He exited to give Wittipol her message to him.

Mrs. Frances Fitzdottrel said to herself, "If Wittipol is the master now of that state and intelligence which I think that he is, surely he will understand me.

"I dare not be more direct because I find already that this officious fellow, my husband's new servant, is a spy my husband has set upon me.

"Yet, if Pug just tells Wittipol my message using my words, Wittipol cannot but know that he is both understood and requited.

"I would not have him think he met a statue, or spoke to someone who was not there, although I remained silent when he spoke to me in my husband's presence."

Pug returned, and she asked him, "What is your news? Have you told him my message?"

"Yes," Pug replied.

"And what does he say?" she asked.

"What does he say?" Pug said, "He says that which I myself would say to you, if I dared.

"He says that you are proud, sweet mistress, and also that you are a little ignorant — that you don't know enough to entertain the good that's proffered to you by him.

"And, pardon me for saying this to one as beautiful as you, he says that you are not all as wise as some true politic — crafty — wife would be, who, having married such a nupson, such a simpleton — my apology to my master — whose face has left to accuse him now, for it confesses him what you can make him, but will yet, out of scruple and a spiced — dainty — conscience, defraud the poor gentleman, or at least delay him in the thing he longs for and makes it his whole study how to compass only a title. If he would just write cuckold as his title, he would have what he deserved."

According to Wittipol — and Pug — Fitzdottrel had a face that accused him of being a fool who deserved to be a cuckold, although he was not yet one, due to the dainty conscience of his wife. If Mrs. Frances Fitzdottrel were like other wives, the ones who were crafty, she would help him get what he wanted: a title. True, the title that he wanted was the title of duke, but she could give him the title that he deserved: the title of cuckold.

Pug continued, "For, look you —"

Mrs. Frances Fitzdottrel thought, *This can be nothing but my husband's plan.*

Pug was not talking to her the way a servant should. A servant would relay Wittipol's message, but Pug was adding that Wittipol's message is what he himself would say to her. Wittipol wanted her to commit adultery with him, and Pug was saying the same thing but about himself. Mrs. Frances Fitzdottrel believed that this was a trap that her husband had set for her.

Pug continued, "— my precious mistress —"

Mrs. Frances Fitzdottrel thought, *It creaks his engine — his trickery creaks. This servant would never dare otherwise to be so saucy if my husband had not put him up to this.*

Pug continued, "— if it were not clearly his worshipful ambition, and the top of it, the very forked top, too" — readers should be thinking of the horned top of a cuckold — "why should he keep you thus walled up in a back room, mistress, never allow you a window opening to the street due to his fear of your becoming pregnant by the eyes with gallants? Why should he forbid you paper, pen, and ink, as if they were rat poison? Why should he search your half pint of muscatel lest a letter be sunk in the pot? And why would he hold your newly laid egg against the fire, lest any charm be written in invisible ink there?"

Lemon juice makes a good invisible ink. When heated, the dried juice turns brown and what is written becomes visible.

Pug continued, "Will you make yourself a benefit from knowing the truth, dear mistress, if I tell the truth to you? I don't do it often!

"I am set over you, employed, indeed, to watch your steps, your looks, even your breaths, and report them to him.

"Now, if you will be a true, right, delicate, sweet mistress, why, we will make a cokes — a fool — of this 'wise' master. We will, my mistress, make of him an absolute fine cokes — and we will openly mock all the deep diligences of such a solemn and effectual ass, an ass to so good purpose as we'll use him.

"I will contrive it so that you shall go to plays, to masques, to meetings, and to feasts.

"For why have all this rigging and fine tackle, mistress — all this fine clothing — if you neat handsome vessels of good sail do not ever and often put forth with your nets abroad into the world? It is your fishing.

"There you shall choose your friends, your servants, lady, your squires of honor."

These friends, servants, and squires of honor would be her lovers.

Pug continued, "I'll convey your letters, fetch answers, do you all the offices that can belong to your blood and beauty.

"And for the variety, when I am inclined, although I am not in due symmetry the man of that proportion, or in rule of medical science of the just complexion, or of that truth of fine fashion in clothes to boast a sovereignty over ladies, yet I know how to do my turns as a lover, sweet mistress."

Pug was offering himself as a lover — for variety — to Mrs. Frances Fitzdottrel. In doing so, he was engaging in false modesty, calling himself a man without a fine body, a fine face, or fine clothes. Actually, the hanged cutpurse whose body Pug had possessed had a fine body and a fine face, and Pug had gotten fine clothes elsewhere.

Pug continued, "Come, kiss —"

"What is this!" Mrs. Frances Fitzdottrel said.

Pug said, "Dear delicate mistress, I am your slave, your little worm that loves you, your fine monkey, your dog, your servant, your pug, that longs to be styled one of your pleasures!"

Thinking that this was a trap and that her husband was watching, Mrs. Frances Fitzdottrel said loudly, "Did you hear all this? Sir, please come out from your hiding place so you can applaud your servant who so well follows your instructions!"

Fitzdottrel entered the room and asked, "What is it, sweetheart? What's the matter?"

"Good man!" his wife said, sarcastically. "You are a stranger to the plot! You did not set your saucy Devil here to tempt your wife with all the insolent uncivil language or action he could vent and express?"

She still believed that he had used Pug to set a trap for her.

Fitzdottrel asked Pug, "Did you do that, Devil?"

Mrs. Frances Fitzdottrel said, "Not you? Weren't you planted in your hole upon the stairs so you could hear him? Or weren't you here, behind the wall hangings? Don't I know your personal character? Did he dare to do it without you giving him directions? That is not possible!"

"You shall see, wife," Fitzdottrel said, "whether he dared to do it on his own, or not, and what it was I directed him to do."

He left, but immediately returned, carrying a cudgel.

"Sweet mistress, are you mad?" Pug asked.

He could guess who the cudgel was for, and he would like to get out of a beating by lying and blaming his mistress for giving false information to her husband.

"You most absolute rogue!" Fitzdottrel said to Pug. "You open and clearly revealed villain! You fiend apparent, you! You declared Hell-hound!"

He began to beat Pug with the cudgel.

"Good sir!" Pug said.

"Good knave, good rascal, and good traitor!" Fitzdottrel said. "Now I find you to be part-devil indeed. Upon the point of trust? In your first charge? The very day of your probation? To tempt your mistress?"

Pug's job had been to keep Fitzdottrel's wife from committing adultery, yet he was attempting to persuade her to commit adultery.

Fitzdottrel said to his wife, "You see, good wedlock — good wife — how I directed him."

"Why, where, sir, were you?" Mrs. Frances Fitzdottrel asked.

If he hadn't been spying on her, then where had he been?

Fitzdottrel paused and then hit Pug again with the cudgel.

He said to Pug, "There is one more blow, for exercise; I told you I would do it."

He had said that he would beat Pug if Pug displeased him. He also had said that he beat his servant for exercise.

Pug replied, "I wish that you were done beating me!"

Fitzdottrel said, "Oh, wife, the rarest, most splendid man!"

He struck Pug again and said, "Yet there's another blow to help you remember the last one."

He said to his wife, "Such a splendid man, wife, is inside! He has his projects, and he vents them. They are the gallantest projects!"

He said to Pug, "Were you tentiginous — horny? Ha? Would you be acting like an incubus, an evil spirit that sleeps with women at night? Did her silks' rustling excite you?"

"Gentle sir!" Pug said.

"Get out of my sight!" Fitzdottrel shouted. "If thy name were not Devil, thou would not stay a minute with me. Go in! Yet stay. Yet go, too. I have decided what I will do; and you shall know it beforehand — as soon as the gentleman has gone, do you hear? I'll help your lisping."

Pug, who had been sputtering, exited.

"Wife, such a man, wife!" Fitzdottrel said. "He has such plots! He will make me a duke! No less, by heaven. You will have six mares to your coach, wife! That's your share. And your coachman will be bald because he shall be bare enough!"

It was the fashion for the coachmen of rich ladies to be bareheaded.

"Don't you laugh," Fitzdottrel added. "We are looking for a place all over the map for me to be duke of. Have faith, and don't be an infidel when it comes to me. You know I am not easily gulled and made a fool of.

"I swear, when I have my millions, I'll make another woman a duchess, if you don't have faith in me."

"You'll have too much, I fear, in these false spirits," Mrs. Frances Fitzdottrel said.

She believed that he would invest too much money in conjurors: Her husband had not yet identified the man he had been talking to.

"Spirits? Oh, no such thing, wife!" Fitzdottrel said. "Wit, mere wit! I'm talking about intelligence and skill. This man defies the devil and all his works!

He does his work by the use of ingenuity and devices, he does! He has his winged plows that go with sails and plow forty acres at once! And he has mills that will spout out water from ten miles away!

"All Crowland is ours, wife; and the fens, from us in Norfolk to the utmost bound of Lincolnshire!"

Crowland was a town in marshy territory in the north of England. Fitzdottrel was hoping to drain the marshes, aka fens, and make a huge profit from the recovered land.

Fitzdottrel continued, "We have viewed it, and measured it within all, by the scale! It is the richest tract of land, love, in the kingdom! There will be made seventeen or eighteen millions, or more, depending on how well it is handled! Therefore think, sweetheart: If thou have a fancy to one place more than another to be duchess of, name it now. I will have it, whatever it costs, if it will be had for money, either here, or in France, or in Italy."

"You have strange fantasies!" his wife replied.

"Where are you, sir?" Merecraft called.

Merecraft and Engine entered the room.

Fitzdottrel said to his wife, "I see thou have no talent in this area of expertise, wife. Go up to thy gallery; go, chuck. Leave us who understand it alone to talk about it."

"Chuck" was a term of endearment, but it need not necessarily be said endearingly.

Mrs. Frances Fitzdottrel exited.

"I think we have found a place to fit you now, sir: Gloucester," Merecraft said.

"Oh no, I'll have nothing to do with Gloucester!" Fitzdottrel said.

"Why not, sir?" Merecraft said.

"It is fatal," Fitzdottrel said.

Many dignitaries of Gloucester had died violently or under suspicious circumstances.

"You are right," Merecraft said. "Spenser, I think, the younger, had his last honor from Gloucester. But he was only an earl."

Hugh le Despenser's father-in-law had been the Earl of Gloucester. When his father-in-law died, Hugh le Despenser was sometimes called the Earl of Gloucester.

"I did not know that, sir," Fitzdottrel said. "But Thomas of Woodstock, I'm sure, was Duke of Gloucester, and he was made away with at Calais, as Duke Humphrey was at Bury. And King Richard III — you know what end he came to."

Thomas of Woodstock, Duke of Gloucester, was murdered in 1397.

Duke Humphrey of Gloucester was the Lord Protector of King Henry VI; he died under suspicious circumstances in 1447.

King Richard III, who was another Duke of Gloucester, died in 1485 in the Battle of Bosworth.

"By my faith, you are knowledgeable in the contents of the historical chronicle, sir," Merecraft said.

"No, I confess I have my history from the playbooks, and I think they're more authentic than the historical chronicle," Fitzdottrel said.

Plays such as William Shakespeare's histories were popular on the stage, but Shakespeare and other playwrights of the time did such things as compress time: Events that took years in real life could seem to take only a few days when presented on the stage. Playwrights also invented characters and ignored facts when convenient for their purposes.

"That's surely true, sir," Engine said.

"What do you say to being duke of this, then?" Fitzdottrel asked.

He said quietly the name of a place.

"No, a noble house lays claim to that," Fitzdottrel said. "I will do no man wrong."

"Then listen to one more proposition," Merecraft said, "and hear it as past exception."

"What's that?" Fitzdottrel asked.

"To be duke of those lands you shall recover. Take your title from there, sir: Duke of the Drowned-lands, or Duke of the Drowned-land."

"Ha! That last has a good sound! I like it well," Fitzdottrel said. "The Duke of Drowned-land!"

"Yes," Engine said. "It's a name like Green-land, sir, if you notice."

"Aye, and drawing thus your honor from the work, you make the reputation of that work greater, and that reputation will stay the longer in your name," Merecraft said.

Every time people heard "the Duke of Drowned-land," they would remember the great task of draining the swampland. Since Fitzdottrel would be the Duke of Drowned-land, the glory of draining the swampland would for a long time be attached to his name.

"That's true," Fitzdottrel said. "Drowned-lands will live in Drowned-land! The memory of Drowned-lands will live in the title of Duke of Drowned-land!"

Merecraft said, "Yes, it will live on in the title when you have no foot of land left, as that must be, sir, one day."

If Fitzdottrel invested Merecraft's schemes, he very well could have no foot of land left one day.

Merecraft continued, "And, even though it tarry in your heirs some forty, fifty descents, yet the longer liver must at last thrust them out of it, if no quirk or quibble in law or odd vice of their own doesn't do it first."

He was saying that eventually the recovered land would pass out of the possession of Fitzdottrel's descendants: Someone else would own it. Perhaps the land would be left to the longer-lived of two people: one of Fitzdottrel's descendants and perhaps the descendant's creditor. If the creditor lived longer, the creditor would possess the recovered land. If the creditor happened to be a lawyer, the lawyer would possess the land.

Merecraft continued, "We see those changes daily. The fair lands that were the client's are the lawyer's now, and those rich manors there of goodman tailor's had once more wood upon them than the yard by which they were measured out for the last purchase."

One of Fitzdottrel's descendants could overspend so much on extravagant clothing that the tailor would end up possessing the land.

"Nature has these vicissitudes. She makes no man a state of perpetuity, sir."

"You're in the right," Fitzdottrel said. "Let's go in, then, and conclude our business."

Pug entered the room.

Seeing Pug, Fitzdottrel said, "Are you in my sight again? I'll talk with you soon."

Fitzdottrel, Merecraft, and Engine exited.

Alone, Pug said to himself, "Surely, he will geld — castrate — me if I stay. Or worse, he will pluck out my tongue. He will do one of the two.

"This fool, there is no trusting him. And to quit him would be a show of contempt against my chief past pardon.

"It was a shrewd disheartening this, at first! Who would have thought a woman so well harnessed, or rather well-caparisoned, indeed, who wears such petticoats and lace to her smocks, broad laces to cover the seams in her stockings (as I see them hang there), and garters that are lost, if she can show them, could have done this? Hell!"

Pug was wondering how Mrs. Frances Fitzdottrel could dress so well and yet be so resistant to committing adultery. Why would a woman dress so well if not to attract someone who would beg a garter as a gift to treasure?

He continued, "Why is she dressed so splendidly? It cannot be to please Duke Dottrel, surely, nor the dull pictures of ancestors that hang in her gallery, nor to please her own dear reflection in her mirror."

A dottrel is a stupid bird.

Pug continued, "Yet that last one may be true: I have known many women to begin their pleasure, but none to end it, there — that last one I consider to be right, as I think about it. Women may, for lack of better company, or lack of company that they think the better, spend an hour, or two, or three, or four, discoursing with their shadow, aka reflection. But surely they have a farther speculation. No woman dressed with so much care and study dresses herself in vain."

According to Pug, any woman who dressed so well and had such a husband must be looking for a lover.

"I'll consider this problem a little more before I leave it, surely."

He exited.

Wittipol and Manly appeared together at the window of Manly's chamber, which was opposite the Fitzdottrels' house. The two buildings were next to each other. Indeed, these two houses were so close together that two people — each leaning out a window in each house — could touch. The window of the Fitzdottrels' house was for a long gallery of pictures where Mrs. Frances Fitzdottrel could walk.

Wittipol intended to talk to Mrs. Frances Fitzdottrel.

"This is better luck than I could imagine," Wittipol said. "This turns out to be thy chamber — I thought that finding a window I could access to get close to the Fitzdottrels' house would be my greatest trouble!"

Remembering the instructions Mrs. Frances Fitzdottrel had given to him through Pug, he said, "This must be the very window and that must be the very room she talked about."

The room was the gallery in the Fitzdottrels' house. Mrs. Frances Fitzdottrel could look out a window of the room and see Manly's window.

"You are right — it is," Manly said. "I now remember that I have often seen there in the gallery a woman, but I never noticed her much. I certainly never looked at her closely."

"Where was your soul, friend?" Wittipol asked.

He could not imagine someone's seeing Mrs. Frances Fitzdottrel and not wanting to look at her closely.

Manly replied, "In faith, but now and then awake to those objects."

Truly, at times he could notice and be greatly affected by the beauty of a woman.

"You claim to," Wittipol said. "Let me not live if I am not in love more with her intelligence that she showed in giving me her instructions for me to go to this window now than with her bodily form, though I have praised that prettily since I saw her and you today."

Wittipol then gave Manly a paper, on which was the copy of the lyrics of a song.

He then said, "Read those lyrics. They'll go with the air — the tune — you love so well. Try them to the note; maybe the music will call her here sooner."

Mrs. Frances Fitzdottrel appeared at her window.

Wittipol said to Manly, "By God's light, she's here! Sing quickly."

Mrs. Frances Fitzdottrel was worried that her instructions to Wittipol to come to the window had not been understood or properly communicated.

She said to herself, "Either Wittipol did not understand Pug, or else Pug was not faithful in the delivery of what I told him to speak. And I am justly paid, I who might have made my profit from his service, but by mistakenly trying to give him secret instructions I have drawn his ill-will upon and done the worse injury to myself."

Manly sang the lyrics Wittipol had given to him:

"*See the chariot at hand here of Love,*

"*Wherein my lady rides!*

"*Each that draws is a swan or a dove,*

"*And well the car Love guides.*

"*As she goes, all hearts do duty*

"*Unto her beauty;*

"*And enamoured, do wish, so they might*

"*But enjoy such a sight,*

"*That they still were to run by her side,*

"*Through swords, through seas, whither she would ride.*"

Mrs. Frances Fitzdottrel said, "What! Music? Then Wittipol may be there — and there he is, to be sure."

Hearing the song, Pug entered the scene.

Seeing Mrs. Frances Fitzdottrel and Wittipol, he said, "Oh, is that the way it is? Is this here the interview between these two? Have I drawn close to you at last, my cunning lady? The devil is an ass! Fooled off, and beaten! The devil made an instrument, and could not scent it!

"Well, since you've shown the malice of a woman to be no less than her true wit and learning, mistress, I'll try if little Pug has the malignity to pay you back, and so get out of the danger he is in. It is not the pain, but the discredit of it. The devil would not keep a body unbeaten!"

Pug now occupied a human body, but he feared most — more than the actual beating — being mocked in Hell for not being successful at keeping that body from being beaten.

Pug exited to find Fitzdottrel.

Mrs. Frances Fitzdottrel stepped to the window, which was open.

The window she was at and the window Wittipol was at were very close together. Many buildings in medieval timber-frame building were jettied. The upper floor of a building projected beyond the floor under it. In the days before air conditioning, windows were often open in good weather.

Mrs. Frances Fitzdottrel and Wittipol could easily touch each other.

Wittipol said to Manly, "Away, fall back. She is coming."

"I'll leave you, sir," Manly said. "You will be the master of my chamber. I have business elsewhere."

He exited.

"Mistress!" Wittipol called.

Mrs. Frances Fitzdottrel came over to him and said, "You make me paint my cheeks, sir."

She meant that she was blushing.

"They're fair colors, lady, and they are natural colors, not artificial cosmetics," Wittipol said.

They were very close together — within touching distance.

He added, "I did receive some commands from you lately, gentle lady, but they were so coded and wrapped in the delivery that I am afraid I may have misinterpreted them, but still I must make suit to be near your grace."

"Who is there with you, sir?" Mrs. Frances Fitzdottrel asked.

"There is no one but myself," he said. "It turned out, lady, that this is a dear friend's lodging, and so good fortune is conspiring with your poor servant's blessed affections to make his wishes come true."

"Who was singing?" Mrs. Frances Fitzdottrel asked.

"My friend was singing, lady, but he's gone because I asked him to leave when I saw you approach the window. You need not fear or doubt him if he were here. He is too much a gentleman to reveal your secrets."

Mrs. Frances Fitzdottrel said, "Sir, if you judge me by this simple action, and by the outward habit — the way it looks — and appearance of easy conformity with your plan, you may with justice say I am a woman, and a strange woman."

A strange woman is an immodest woman. Some strange women are prostitutes.

"But when you shall please to bring but that concurrence of my fortune to memory, which today yourself did urge, it may beget some favor like an excuse, though none like reason."

She meant that if he would remember the words he had spoken to her earlier, he would likely excuse her actions now, even if they seemed out of line with reason.

These are among the words Wittipol had spoken when he was speaking as if he were her:

"*But sir, you seem a gentleman of virtue no less than of good birth, and one who in every way looks as he were of too good quality to entrap a credulous woman, or betray her.*"

Certainly Wittipol's actions seemed out of line with the description of his looks: He had been trying to convince her to commit adultery.

Responding to the notion that her actions were out of line with reason, Wittipol said, "Reason has no part in your actions, my tuneful, sweet-voiced mistress? Then surely Love has no reason, and Beauty has no reason, and Nature is not violated in both Love and Beauty. You speak at once with all the gentle tongues of Reason, Love, Beauty, and Nature."

According to Wittipol, it was completely in accordance with Reason that she commit adultery with him — and also completely in accordance with Love, Beauty, and Nature.

He continued, "I thought I had enough removed already that scruple from your breast, and left you all reason, when, through my morning's perspective, I showed you a man so beyond excuse that he is the cause for why anything is to be done upon him, and nothing that injures him is to be called a misplaced injury."

In other words, he had used a perspective — a metaphorical microscope — to help her closely examine her husband and realize that he was such a man that any kind of evil could be done to him and no one could say that it was undeserved.

Wittipol continued, "I rather had hope now to show you how Love by his intimate accesses grows more natural, and what was done this morning with such force was but then devised to serve the present."

He grew more familiar in his courtship and intimate accesses, playing with her breasts, kissing her hands, etc.

These are liberties indeed, and Mrs. Frances Fitzdottrel's husband had definitely let her know earlier that she was not to allow Wittipol to touch her. What's going on here? Possibly 1) she was sexually attracted to Wittipol, 2) she was rebelling against her husband, 3) she was manipulating Wittipol because she wanted him to do something for her, or 4) some combination of the above.

Wittipol continued, "Since Love has the honor to approach these sister-swelling breasts, and touch this soft and rosy hand, he has the skill to draw their nectar forth with kissing, and could make more wanton leaps from this brave promontory down to this valley" — he moved a hand from a nipple toward her vulva — "than the nimble deer could play the hopping sparrow about these nets, and could play the sporting squirrel in these crisped, tightly curled groves" — he was referring to her pubic hair.

Deer can leap, sparrows can hop, squirrels can enjoy entertainment, but Love has its own action that outperforms each of these others.

He continued, "Love can bury himself in every silkworm's cocoon that is here unraveled."

In a non-aroused state, the walls of the vagina touch each other. In a sexually aroused state, the clitoris, labia minora, labia majora, and vagina swell as blood rushes to these areas. It is as if the vulva is opening like a flower.

"Love can run into the snare that every hair is.

"Love can cast into a curl to catch a Cupid flying.

"Love can bathe himself in milk and roses here, and dry himself there.

"Love can warm his cold hands to play with this smooth, round, and well-turned chin, as with the billiard ball.

"Love can roll on these lips, the banks of love, and there at once both plant and gather kisses.

"Lady, shall I, with what I have made today here, call all sense to wonder, and all faith to sign the mysteries revealed in your bodily form? And will Love pardon me the blasphemy I uttered when I said a looking-glass could speak this beauty, or that fools had power to judge it?"

He then sang:

"Do but look on her eyes! They do light —
"All that Love's world comprises!
"Do but look on her hair! It is bright
"As Love's star [Venus] when it rises!

"Do but mark [look closely], her forehead's smoother
"Than words that soothe her!
"And from her arched brows, such a grace
"Sheds itself through the face,
"As alone, there triumphs to the life,
"All the gain, all the good, of the elements' strife!
"Have you seen but a bright lily grow
"Before rude hands have touched it?
"Have you marked but the fall of the snow
"Before the soil has smutched [smudged] it?
"Have you felt the wool of the beaver?
"Or swan's down, ever?
"Or have smelt of the bud of the briar?
"Or the nard [aromatic ointment] in the fire?
"Or have tasted the honeybag of the bee?
"Oh, so white! Oh, so soft! Oh, so sweet is she!"

Fitzdottrel appeared behind his wife.

Pug appeared on the street below the two buildings.

Fitzdottrel said to himself, "Is she so, sir?"

He meant: Is my wife attempting to be unfaithful to me?

He added to himself, "And I will keep her so, if I know how, or can."

He meant that he would keep making her attempts to be unfaithful to him unsuccessful.

He added to himself, "I'll go no farther than what the wit — intelligence and skill — of man will do."

He may have meant that the wit — intelligence and skill — of man would be enough to keep his wife from committing adultery.

Or he may have meant that he would attempt to keep her faithful to him, but he would do only what it was possible for him to do. If so, he believed that another woman could replace his wife.

He added to himself, "At this window she shall no more be buzzed at. You can bet on it."

He then said out loud to his wife, "If you are sweetmeats, wedlock, or sweet flesh, all's one and the same to me. I do not love this hum about you. A fly-blown wife is not so proper."

He was comparing his wife — whom he called "wedlock" — to sweets or meat that flies were swarming around.

He ordered her, "Go inside!"

She moved inside the room, away from the window, but Wittipol could still see her and she could still see him.

Fitzdottrel said from his window, "As for you, sir, look to hear from me."

These words were the way a traditional challenge to a duel began.

"So I do, sir," Wittipol replied.

Wittipol was ready to fight a duel with Fitzdottrel.

"No, but in other terms," Fitzdottrel said.

Fitzdottrel was not ready to fight a duel with Wittipol.

Fitzdottrel continued, "There's no man offers this to my wife unless he pays for it."

"I have done that, sir," Wittipol said.

He meant that he had paid with a cloak.

"Nay, then, I tell you, you are —" Fitzdottrel began.

Wittipol asked, "What am I, sir?"

"Why, that I'll think about, when I have cut your throat!"

"Bah, you are an ass," Wittipol said.

"I am resolved on it, sir —" Fitzdottrel began.

Fitzdottrel meant that he was resolved on cutting Wittipol's throat.

"I think you are!" Wittipol interrupted.

Wittipol meant that Fitzdottrel was resolved on being an ass.

Fitzdottrel continued, "— to call you to a reckoning."

"Go away, you broker's block, you property!" Wittipol said, hitting him.

A broker's block or property was a mannequin on which clothing was displayed. Wittipol was referring to Fitzdottrel's custom of renting fine but used clothing.

Fitzdottrel said, "By God's light, if you strike me, I'll strike your mistress."

He hit his wife, and then he and his wife exited.

Furious, Wittipol said, "Oh! I could shoot my eyes at him for that, now, or leave my teeth in him, if they were cuckold's poison enough to kill him!

"What prodigious, blind, and most wicked change of fortune's this? I have no breath of patience — all my veins swell, and my muscles start at the unfairness of it. I shall break, break!"

He exited.

Alone, Pug said to himself, "This I did for the malice of it, and so that my revenge may pass!"

He had caused Wittipol to become very angry at Fitzdottrel; if Wittipol were to beat Fitzdottrel, then Pug would have revenge for Fitzdottrel's beating him. In addition, Mrs. Frances Fitzdottrel had been responsible for Pug being beaten in the first place, and he had gotten revenge on her by stopping her meeting with Wittipol.

"But now my conscience tells me I have profited the cause of Hell but little in breaking off their loves, which, if some other act of mine doesn't repair this damage, I shall hear ill of in my account."

Pug could get in trouble in Hell for interfering with the love of Mrs. Frances Fitzdottrel and Wittipol. He had interfered in a love that could have led to adultery.

Fitzdottrel and his wife came outside and stood near Pug.

"Oh, bird!" Fitzdottrel said. "Could you do this? Against me? And at this time, now? When I was so employed, wholly for you, drowned in my care — more than the land I swear I have hope that I will win — to make you peerless? I have been working to get footmen for you, fine-paced ushers, and pages to serve you and bend their knees respectfully to you.

"I have been working to decide what knight's wife will bear your train, and I have been working so that you can sit with your four women in council, and receive news from foreign parts, and I have been working so you can dress yourself perfectly in every detail!

"You've almost turned my good affection away from you, soured my sweet thoughts, all my pure purposes. I could now find it in my very heart to make another lady duchess and depose you.

"Well, go inside."

His wife went inside.

Fitzdottrel said to Pug, "Devil, you have redeemed everything. I forgive you. And I'll do you good."

The redemption of a devil from Hell is unusual.

Pug exited.

— 2.8 —

Merecraft and Engine came outside and talked to Fitzdottrel.

Merecraft asked, "Why do you have these excursions away from business? Where have you been, sir?"

"I have been where I have been vexed a little, with a trifle!" Fitzdottrel said.

"Oh, sir!" Merecraft said. "No trifles must trouble your grave head, now that it is growing to be great."

Fitzdottrel's head could grow great. He could become big-headed because of pride in his imagined future success. Also, he was in danger of acquiring the horns of a cuckold.

Merecraft continued, "You must be above all those things."

"So I will," Fitzdottrel said.

"Now you are moving toward becoming a lord, you must put off the man, sir," Merecraft said.

"He says the truth," Engine said.

They were telling Fitzdottrel that he need not act like an ordinary man any more, by which they meant he did not have to observe such things as humility and courtesy.

"You must do nothing as you have done it heretofore," Merecraft said. "You must not know or greet any man —"

Engine interrupted, "— who was your bedfellow the other month."

"Bedfellow" here meant "intimate friend," although unmarried people of the same sex could share a bed without causing gossip in this society.

"The other month?" Merecraft said. "The other week."

People experiencing a sudden rise in social status often shake off their old friends.

Merecraft continued, "Thou don't know the privileges, Engine, that follow that title, nor how swiftly they come with the title. Today, when he has put on his lord's face once, then —"

"Sir, concerning these things I shall do well enough," Fitzdottrel said. "I can act like a lord — don't fear that I cannot.

"But then, my wife is such an unpredictable, uncooperative thing! She'll never learn how to conduct herself like a duchess! I don't understand her at all."

"Best have her taught, sir," Merecraft said.

"Where?" Fitzdottrel said. "Are there any schools for ladies? Is there an academy for women? I do know for men there was; I learned in one myself how to perform courtly bows and military drills."

Engine whispered to Merecraft, "Sir, do you remember the idea you had — concerning the Spanish gown, at home?"

Merecraft whispered back, "Ha! I thank thee with all my heart, dear Engine."

Merecraft turned to Fitzdottrel and said, "Sir, there is a certain lady here about the town, an English widow, who has recently travelled, but she's called the Spaniard, because she came most recently from Spain, and wears Spanish clothing.

"She is such a splendid woman! All our women here who are of spirit and fashion flock to her, as to their president, their law, their canon, more than they ever did to oracle Forman."

Doctor Forman was a necromancer who claimed, among other things, to be able to find lost treasure. Women especially flocked to him.

Merecraft continued, "Such rare recipes she has, sir, for the face, such oils, such tinctures, such pomades, such perfumes, medicines, essential oils, etc.

"And she is such a mistress of behavior! She knows, from the duke's daughter to the doxy, what is their just due, and no more than what is their just due."

A doxy is a slut.

"Oh, sir!" Fitzdottrel said. "You please me in this more than my own greatness. Where is she? Let us have her."

"Be patient," Merecraft said. "We must find a means for you to meet her and think about how you two can become acquainted —"

"Good sir, set about it," Fitzdottrel said.

"We must think about how first," Merecraft said.

"Oh, I do not love to wait for a thing, when I have a mind to have it," Fitzdottrel said. "You do not know me if you want me to wait."

"Your wife must send some pretty token to her, with a compliment, and ask to be received in her good graces," Merecraft said. "All the great ladies do it —"

"She shall! She shall!" Fitzdottrel said. "What pretty token would be best?"

"Some little trifle," Merecraft said. "I would not have it be any great matter, sir — a diamond ring of forty or fifty pounds would do it handsomely; and be a gift fit for your wife to send, and fit for the Spanish lady to take."

"I'll go and tell my wife about it right now," Fitzdottrel said.

He exited.

"Why, this is going well!" Merecraft said to Engine. "The Spanish clothes we've already got, but where's this lady? If we could get a witty boy now, Engine, that would be an excellent joke. I could instruct him to the true height. Anything takes this dottrel."

There was no Spanish lady; this was just another con that seemed to be about to pay off immediately with a diamond ring worth forty or fifty pounds. Fitzdottrel was a dottrel — a foolish bird — whom it was easy to take advantage of.

Engine said, "Why, sir, one of the players will be your best female impersonator."

The players were theatrical actors. In this society, women did not act in the theater. Boys played the roles of women.

"No, there's no trusting them to keep it secret," Merecraft said. "They'll talk about it, and tell their playwrights."

"So what if they do?" Engine said. "The jest will suit the stage. But there are some of them who are very honest lads. There's Dick Robinson, who is a very pretty fellow, and who comes often to the chamber of a gentleman who is a friend of mine."

Dick Robinson was a boy actor who played women's roles on stage.

Engine continued, "We had the merriest supper of it there, one night! The gentleman's landlady invited my friend to a feast for friends. Now my friend, sir, brought Dick Robinson, dressed like a lawyer's wife, among them all — I lent him the clothes — but to see him act out the role, and lay the law, and act refined, and drink to them, and then talk bawdy, and send frolics! Oh, your laughter would have burst your buttons, or would not have left you with an unsplit seam in your clothing."

Frolics were humorous or amatory verses written on paper and wrapped around sweetmeats and placed in bowls. During a feast, guests would send frolics to each other.

Sweetmeats are sweet delicacies such as bonbons, candied fruit, sugarplums, sugar-covered nuts, or balls or sticks of candy.

"They say he's an ingenious youth," Merecraft said.

"Oh, sir!" Engine said. "And he dresses himself the best! Beyond forty of your real ladies! Have you ever seen him?"

"No, I seldom see those trifles," Merecraft said. "But do you think that we may have him pretend to be the Spanish lady?"

"Sir, the young gentleman friend I tell you of can get him to perform the role," Engine said. "Shall I ask my young gentleman friend?"

"Yes, do it," Merecraft said.

Engine exited.

Fitzdottrel returned and said, "By God's light, I cannot get my wife to part with a ring on any terms, and yet the sullen monkey has two."

"It is against reason that you should urge her to give up one of her rings, sir," Merecraft said. "Send to a goldsmith. Don't let her lose by giving up a ring."

"How does she lose by it?" Fitzdottrel asked. "Isn't it for her?'

By giving up the ring, his wife would gain the friendship of the Spanish lady. This was a gain — so Fitzdottrel thought.

"Make it your own bounty," Merecraft said. "It will have the better success. What is a matter of fifty pounds to you, sir?"

"I've only a hundred pieces to show here, and that I would not break —"

Merecraft interrupted, "You shall have credit, sir. I'll send a note to my goldsmith."

Trains, Merecraft's manservant, entered the room.

Merecraft said, "Here my manservant comes. He can carry my note to my goldsmith."

He then said, "How are things now, Trains? What birds?"

"What birds?" meant "What's up?"

Knowing Merecraft, the slang comes from hunting — the birds were prey to be shot just like Fitzdottrel was prey to be cheated.

"Your cousin Everill met me, and he has beaten me because I would not tell him where you were," Trains answered. "I think he has dogged me and followed to the house, too."

"Well, you shall go out at the back door, then, Trains," Merecraft said. "You must get Gilthead the goldsmith here by some means."

"That is impossible!" Trains said.

"Tell him we have venison," Fitzdottrel said. "I'll give him a piece, and send his wife a pheasant."

Fitzdottrel exited.

"A forest of deer will not persuade him to come until those forty pounds you most recently got from him are paid back," Trains said. "He makes more noise about that petty sum than he does about your bond of six and statute of eight hundred."

A statute was a loan whose collateral was land. If the loan were not paid back, the creditor could legally seize the bound land of the debtor.

"Tell him we'll hedge in that," Merecraft said.

That meant that he would include the forty pounds he owed in a larger debt that had better security.

He added, "Talk up Fitzdottrel to him. Say that Fitzdottrel's net worth is twice what it really is; make him a man of metal."

The metal he had in mind was gold.

"That will not be necessary," Trains said. "Fitzdottrel's bond is current enough. He has good credit."

CHAPTER 3

— 3.1 —

Gilthead the goldsmith and Plutarchus talked together. Plutarchus was Gilthead's son.

"All this is to make you a gentleman," Gilthead said. "I'll have you learn, son. Why have I placed you with Sir Paul Eitherside except for the purpose of having you learn enough law that you can keep what is your own? Besides, he is a justice here in the town; and by dwelling, son, with him you shall learn in a single year what shall be worth twenty years of supporting you at Oxford or at Cambridge, or sending you to the Inns of Court or to France.

"I am called for now in haste by Master Merecraft to give credit to Master Fitzdottrel, a (financially) good man — I've inquired about him: He has eighteen hundred pounds a year, and his reputation is (financially) good for a diamond ring that costs forty pounds but will not be worth thirty pounds — that's ten pounds we've gained. And this is to make you a gentleman!"

"Oh, but good father, you trust too much!" Plutarchus said. "You give too much credit!"

"Boy, boy, we live by finding fools to be trusted with credit," Gilthead said. "Our shop-books are our pastures, our corn-grounds. We lay them open for fools to come into, and when we have them there we drive them up into one of our two pounds, the Counters, straightaway. And this is to make you a gentleman!"

The Counters were pounds — prisons — for people who could not pay their debts. Gilthead would get fools to run up debt, bleed them dry with high interest, and send them to prison still owing him money. But the money Gilthead got went for a good cause, he thought: It would make his son a gentleman.

He continued, "We citizens never trust someone with credit but we cheat, for if our debtors pay, we cheat them with our high interest, and if they do not pay, then we cheat ourselves. But that's a hazard everyone must run who hopes to make his son a gentleman."

"I do not wish to be a gentleman, truly, father," Plutarchus said. "In a generation or two, we come to be just in their — the fools' — state, fit to be cheated like them.

"And I would rather have tarried in your trade, for since the gentry scorn the city so much, I think we should in time, holding together, and marrying in our own tribes, as they say, have gotten an Act of Common Council authorizing us legally to cheat them out of *rerum natura*."

"*Rerum natura*" is Latin for "the nature of things"; Plutarchus was using it to mean "everything."

The Roman philosopher Lucretius wrote a work he titled *De Rerum Natura*, or *Concerning the Nature of Things*.

Gilthead said, "Aye, if we had a legislative act first to forbid the marrying of our wealthy heirs to them, and to forbid daughters from having such lavish portions — that ruins everything."

Gentry who lacked money could become wealthy again by marrying someone who had much money — for example, rich Jewish daughters.

"And such practices make us a mongrel breed, father," Plutarchus said. "And when they have your money, then they laugh at you, or kick you down the stairs. I cannot abide them. I would prefer to have them cheated, but not trusted with credit."

Merecraft and Fitzdottrel entered the room in which Gilthead and Plutarchus, his son, were talking.

"Oh, has he come?" Merecraft said. "I knew he would not fail me."

He said quietly, "Welcome, good Gilthead. I must have you do a noble gentleman a courtesy here, in a mere trifle, some pretty ring or jewel, of fifty or threescore pounds — make it a hundred, and hedge in the last forty that I owe you, and your own price for the ring."

Merecraft wanted the most recent forty pounds he owed Gilthead to be made a part of the loan that Fitzdottrel would get from Gilthead. That way, Fitzdottrel would be the guarantor of the loan. If Merecraft were to default on the loan — have no doubt he would — Fitzdottrel would be legally responsible for paying back the loan.

More loudly, Merecraft continued talking to Gilthead, "He's a good man, sir, and you may perhaps see him become a great man. He is likely to bestow hundreds and thousands of pounds on you, if you can humor him by giving him credit now. A great prince he will be shortly. What do you say?"

"In truth, sir, I cannot," Gilthead said. "It has been a long vacation with us —"

The Inns of Court took a long vacation from August 13 to October 23. The vacation cut down on profits for many shopkeepers such as Gilthead.

Fitzdottrel interrupted, "A long vacation from what, I ask thee? From wit and intelligence? Or honesty? Those are your citizens' long vacations."

Angry at not immediately being granted credit, he walked away and looked out a window, ignoring the others.

Plutarchus whispered to Gilthead, his father, "Good father, do not trust them. "

"Nay, Tom Gilthead," Merecraft said. "Fitzdottrel will not buy a courtesy and beg it; he'll rather pay than beg."

Fitzdottrel had money; he did not need to beg for it.

Merecraft continued, "If you do for him, you must do cheerfully. His credit, sir, is not yet prostitute."

If Fitzdottrel spent enough time with Merecraft and his fellow con artists, Fitzdottrel's credit would become prostitute.

Merecraft then asked Gilthead, "Who's this? Thy son? A handsome youth. What's his name?"

"Plutarchus, sir," Plutarchus answered for his father.

"Plutarchus!" Merecraft said. "How did you get that name?"

Gilthead answered for his son, "The year, sir, that I begot him, I bought Plutarch's *Lives*, and fell so in love with the book that I called my son by his name, in the hope he would be like Plutarch and write the lives of our great men."

"In the city?" Merecraft asked. "And are you raising him there?"

"His mind, sir, lies much to that way," Gilthead replied.

"Why then, he is in the right way," Merecraft said.

"But now I had rather get him a good wife, and plant him in the country, there to use the blessing I shall leave him," Gilthead said.

"Not a good idea!" Merecraft said. "If thou do that, thou shall lose the laudable means thou have at home, here, to advance him and make him a young alderman!"

Merecraft guessed that he would get in Plutarchus' good graces by advocating that Plutarchus be allowed to stay in the city. Also, if Plutarchus were to live in the country after receiving his father's financial blessing, Merecraft would not be able to borrow money from him.

He continued, "Buy him a military captain's position in the Artillery Company, for shame; and let him go into the world early, and with his military scarlet ostrich-plume and military scarfs worn across his chest march through Cheapside, or along Cornhill, and by the virtue of those military decorations draw down a wife there from a window worth ten thousand pounds! Get him the book for learning military drills and get him some soldier men made of lead to set upon a table, in case his mistress should chance to come by, so that he may draw her in and show her Finsbury battles."

Military training exercises, including mock battles, took place at Finsbury, a London district.

Gilthead said, "I have placed him with Justice Eitherside, to learn as much law —"

"As thou has conscience," Merecraft said. "Come, come, thou are wronging pretty Plutarchus, who has not received his name for nothing, but was born to train the youth of London in the military truth. That way his genius lies."

Hearing a noise, he looked up and said, "My cousin Everill!"

Everill entered the room and said, "Oh, are you here, sir? Please, let us whisper together."

He took Merecraft aside so they could talk quietly and privately together.

Plutarchus said to Gilthead, "Father, dear father, trust him, if you love me."

He had changed his mind about Merecraft. Perhaps the military life appealed to him. Certainly staying in the city did. Merecraft's description of military life involved staying in the city.

Trusting Merecraft involved trusting Fitzdottrel; Merecraft would do everything possible to make Fitzdottrel responsible for paying back any loans.

"Why, I intend to trust him, boy," Gilthead said, "but what I do must not come easily from me. We must deal with courtiers, boy, as courtiers deal with us. If I have a business there with any of them, why, I must wait, I'm sure of it, son; and although my lord dispatch me, yet his 'worshipful' manservant will keep me for his entertainment a month or two, to show me with my fellow citizens. I must make his train long and full, for one quarter, and help the spectacle of his greatness."

The "courtier" was Merecraft, and the "lord" was Fitzdottrel. Merecraft did not treat Gilthead well, as could be seen by the way he talked to him. Therefore, although Gilthead was willing to do business with Fitzdottrel, he would hold off a while because Merecraft was the middleman.

Gilthead treated courtiers, including the ones he lent money, the way they treated him. He made them wait to get a loan, and they made him wait to be repaid for the loan. True, he made interest as long as the loan was made, but the courtiers made him jump through metaphorical hoops as he waited to be repaid.

Or, if the lord were the one getting the loan, then the lord's manservant — the courtier — would make him wait. Gilthead would be joining others in the lord's retinue as he waited, and the lord — and the courtier — would seem to be a great man because of the retinue.

Gilthead continued, "There nothing is done at once but injuries, boy — and they come headlong! All great men's good turns don't move, or they move very slowly."

"Yet, sweet father, trust him," Plutarchus said.

"Well, I will think about it," Gilthead said.

He and his son then talked together quietly.

Meanwhile, Everill said to Merecraft, "Come, you must do it, sir. I'm ruined, otherwise, and your Lady Tailbush has sent for me to come to dinner, and all my clothes are pawned. I had sent out this morning, before I heard you had come to town, some twenty of my epistles, and no one return —"

The epistles were letters begging for money.

Merecraft interrupted and told Everill about his faults:

"Why, I have told you about this. This comes from wearing fancy clothes of scarlet, gold lace, and cut-works. Your fine gartering! With your blown roses on your shoes, cousin! And your eating pheasant and godwit — another fowl that is a delicacy — here in London. And your haunting the Globes and Mermaids — theaters and taverns — and squeezing in with lords always at the table! And affecting lechery in velvet — you consort with expensive whores who wear velvet!

"Instead, you could have contented yourself with cheese, salt-butter, and a pickled herring in the Low Countries — there you could have worn inexpensive cloth such as fustian! You could have been satisfied with a sexual leap on your host's daughter in the garrison — a wench you could have bought with the small coin that is called a stoler! Or you could have been satisfied with a sexual leap on your sutler's wife, in the leaguer, whom you could pay with two small coins that are called blanks!"

A sutler sells provisions to the soldiers in a military camp, aka leaguer.

Merecraft continued, "You never then would have run upon this low point that forced you to write your begging letters and send out your privy seals that thus have frightened off all your acquaintances so that they shun you at a distance, worse than you shun the debt collectors!"

Everill grumbled, "A pox upon you! I didn't come to you for advice. I lack money."

"You do not think about what you owe me already?" Merecraft asked.

"I?" Everill said. "They owe you who intend to pay you. I'll be sworn I never meant it."

This sounds as if he never meant to repay Merecraft the debt he owed him, but perhaps he meant: I never meant to reach this low point. Most likely, he meant the first one.

Everill continued, "Come, you will make money with a project."

He then said threateningly, "I shall ruin your practice for this month if you don't help me. You know me."

Everill could inform people such as Fitzdottrel that Merecraft was a con man.

"Yes, you have a very 'sweet' nature!" Merecraft said.

"Well, that's all one," Everill said. "Who cares?"

"You'll leave this empire one day," Merecraft said. "You will not ever have this tribute paid, despite your scepter of the sword!"

He was saying that he would not be intimidated. Everill was ordering him around as if Everill were an emperor, but he was gaining his power with a sword — threats — instead of with a scepter — rightful rule.

"Tie up your wit," Everill said, "and don't provoke me —"

"Will you, sir, help me in doing what I shall provoke another to do for you?" Merecraft asked.

Merecraft did not want to give Everill money, but he was willing to con someone into giving Everill money. To do so, he needed Everill's help.

"I cannot tell; try me," Everill said. "I think I am not so utterly of an ore un-to-be-melted, but I can do myself good on occasions."

"Strike in then, and do your part," Merecraft said.

Merecraft and Everill then went over to Fitzdottrel.

Merecraft said to him, "Master Fitzdottrel, if I transgress in point of manners, give me your best interpretation of my conduct. I must beg for my freedom from your affairs this day."

Merecraft began to gather his coat and hat and papers.

"What is it, sir?" Fitzdottrel said.

"I need to leave to help in this gentleman's affairs. He is my kinsman —"

"You'll not do me that affront, sir," Fitzdottrel said.

He was eager to quickly rise in society and to quickly become very wealthy.

"I am sorry you should so interpret my action as an affront," Merecraft said. "But, sir, it has to do with his being invested in a new office he has stood for a long time: Master of the Dependences!"

A dependence was a quarrel that needed to be settled. Many quarrels were settled through duels, which King James I of England opposed.

As he would now say, Merecraft wanted to set up an Office of Dependency, in which Everill would be the chief official. According to Merecraft, as he would soon say, this was one of his projects: Like other of his projects, it sounded somewhat plausible but had little chance of actually being set up and little chance of actually working.

Merecraft said, "The Office of Dependency is a place of my own design, too, sir, and it has met with much opposition; but the state, now, sees the great necessity of it, as after all their writing and their speaking against duels, they have erected it."

Merecraft continued, "Everill's official charter has been drawn up — for since there will be differences daily, between gentlemen, and since the roaring manner has grown offensive, with the result that those few we call the civil men of the sword abhor the vain and foolish bragging, they shall refer now hither for their process. And such as trespass against the rule of court are to be fined —"

Roaring boys were young men — bullies — who engaged in much arguing and dueling. Many roaring boys were in London.

Presumably, rather than settling quarrels through illegal dueling, which King James I had outlawed, gentlemen who had disagreements would go to the Office of Dependency and have their quarrels legally settled there. Fitzdottrel would learn that he must settle his affairs before settling his quarrel, so likely the way to settle quarrels was through legal duels approved by the Office of Dependency.

"Truly, a pretty place!" Fitzdottrel said.

"A kind of arbitrary court it will be, sir," Merecraft said.

"I shall have a case for it, I believe, before long," Fitzdottrel said. "I had a distaste."

His distaste was his quarrel with Wittipol.

"But now, sir," Merecraft said, "my learned counsel, they must have a feeling — a bribe. They'll part, sir, with no books — written grants of privileges — unless the hand-gout be oiled, and I must furnish the oil."

The hand-gout is a tight fist.

Merecraft continued, "If it concerns money, they come to me straightaway: I am a precious-metal mine, mint, and treasury, and I supply all."

He asked Everill, "How much is it? A hundred pounds?"

It was time for Everill to play his part in conning Fitzdottrel.

He replied, "No, the greedy harpy now insists on a hundred pieces."

A hundred pieces was ten percent more than a hundred pounds. A pound is twenty shillings; a piece is twenty-two shillings.

"Why, he must have them, if he insists," Merecraft said.

He then said to Fitzdottrel, "Tomorrow, sir, will equally serve your needs, and therefore let me obtain your consent that you will yield me time to help a poor gentleman in his distresses because of his affairs' urgency—"

"By no means!" Fitzdottrel said.

"I must get him this money, and will —" Merecraft said.

"Sir, I protest, I'd rather stand as the guarantor for the money myself than you should leave me," Fitzdottrel said.

"Oh, good sir," Merecraft said, "do you think so coarsely of our manners that we would, for any need of ours, be pressed to take it, although you would be pleased to offer it?"

He was pretending not to want Fitzdottrel to be the guarantor for the loan.

"Why, by heaven, I mean it!" Fitzdottrel said.

"I can never believe less," Merecraft said. "But we, sir, must preserve our dignity, as you do publish — make public — yours. By your fair leave, sir."

He pretended to start to leave.

"As I am a gentleman," Fitzdottrel said, "if you intend to leave me now, or if you refuse me, I will not think you love and respect me."

"Sir, I honor you," Merecraft said. "And with just reason, for these noble notes of the nobility you pretend to."

The "noble notes" included the offer to be the guarantor of the money that Merecraft said that Everill needed.

The word "pretend" means "has a claim to," in addition to its regular meaning. Merecraft knew that Fitzdottrel had no real chance of becoming a duke; all he had was a real chance of losing his wealth.

Merecraft continued, "But sir, I would like to know why you would do this — he is a stranger. What is your reason for helping him?"

Everill whispered to Merecraft, "You'll mar all with your fineness."

Everill wanted to take the money and run, but Merecraft was prolonging the time that he would accept Fitzdottrel's offer to be the guarantor of the loan.

"Why, sir, that's all one — it wouldn't matter if it were only my fancy," Fitzdottrel said. "But I have a business that perhaps I'd have brought to his office."

"Oh, sir!" Merecraft said. "I have no objections to your being guarantor, then, if he can be made profitable to you."

"Yes, and it shall be one of my ambitions to have it the first business," Fitzdottrel said. "Can I do that?"

"As long as you intend to make it a perfect business," Everill said.

The word "business" meant "a private quarrel."

"I'll do that, I assure you," Fitzdottrel said. "Show me immediately what to do."

"Sir, it is important that the first be a perfect business, for Everill's own honor," Merecraft said.

Everill said, "Yes, and for the reputation, too, of my office."

The legal term "perfect" meant "enforceable by law." The private business, aka enforceable-by-law quarrel, would have to be one that was clearly suitable to be resolved — and would be resolved — by the Office of Dependency. That way, people would see that the Office of Dependency worked, and King James I and other VIPs would support it.

"Why, why do I take this course otherwise?" Fitzdottrel said. "I am not altogether an ass, good gentlemen. Wherefore should I consult you? Do you think to make a song and dance of it? Get to the point. What's your procedure for resolving quarrels? Tell us."

"Do, satisfy him," Merecraft said to Everill. "Tell him the whole course of action."

"First," Everill said, "by request, or otherwise, you offer your business to the court, wherein you crave the judgment of the Master and the Assistants."

"Well, that's done," Fitzdottrel said. "Now what do you do next?"

"We straightaway, sir, have recourse to the source of the business," Everill said. "We visit the ground — that is, we examine the root causes of the quarrel, and so we see whether or not it is suitable for resolution by the Office of Dependency. If we find by our estimate that it is likely to prove to be a sullen and black business, that it is incorrigible and the parties are unable to negotiate a resolution, then we file it as a dependence."

Fitzdottrel said, "So, it is filed. What follows? I love the order of these things."

Everill said, "We then advise the party, if he is a man of means and possessions, that forthwith he settle his estate and put his affairs in order — or if he does not, at least that he says that he intends to do it. For by that the world takes notice that it now is a dependence. And this we call, sir, publication."

"Publication" means "public notification." In this society, however, "publication" also meant "confiscation." Merecraft and Everill would love to confiscate Fitzdottrel's wealth for their own use.

"Very sufficient!" Fitzdottrel said. "After publication, what's next?"

Everill said, "Then we begin our legal process, which can be done in different ways: either by chartel, sir, or by ore-tenus — that is, either by written challenge or by word of mouth. Then the challenger and challengee, or — using Spaniard words — your *provocador* and *provocado*, have their different courses of action —"

"I have enough information about it," Fitzdottrel said. "For a hundred pieces? Yes, for two hundred underwrite me, do. Your man will take my bond?"

"That he will, to be sure," Merecraft said.

Merecraft said quietly to Fitzdottrel, "But these same citizens, they are such sharks! There's an old debt of forty pounds I gave my word as guarantor — I did it for one who has run away to the Bermudas, and he will hook in that or he will not take your bond."

The citizen was Gilthead. Merecraft was trying to con Fitzdottrel into being the guarantor of the debt of forty pounds by saying that Gilthead would not lend Fitzdottrel any money unless Fitzdottrel also assumed the debt of forty pounds. This was Merecraft's way of hedging the debt — Fitzdottrel's credit was much better than his.

Fitzdottrel said quietly, "Why, let him. That and the ring, and a hundred pieces, will all just make two hundred pounds?"

Merecraft said quietly, "No more, sir."

In his mind, Merecraft may have thought, *No. More, sir.* He wanted to take Fitzdottrel for more than two hundred pounds.

He added, "What ready arithmetic you have!"

He then said to Gilthead, "Do you hear? A pretty morning's work for you, this! Do it. You shall have twenty pounds out of it."

Twenty pounds would be ten percent interest on a loan of two hundred pounds.

"Twenty pieces?" Gilthead asked.

He wanted more interest.

"Good father, do it," Plutarchus urged.

"You will hook still?" Merecraft said. "You will fish for more money? Well, show us your ring. You could not have done this now with gentleness at first? If you had, we might have thanked you. But instead of dealing with gentleness, you groan as if you were having a painful defecation, and your courtesies come from you as if you were passing a hard stool, and they stink!

"A man may draw your teeth out easier than your money.

"Come, if little Gilthead here did not have a better nature than you" — he squeezed Plutarchus' lips, which in this society was a friendly gesture — "I would never love him, I who could squeeze his lips off, now."

He then asked Plutarchus, "Wasn't thy mother a gentlewoman?"

"Yes, sir," Plutarchus replied.

"And she went to the court at Christmas and St. George's tide? And she lent the lords' men necklaces?" Merecraft asked.

"Of gold, and pearl, sir," Plutarchus replied.

"I knew thou must take after somebody other than your father," Merecraft said. "That could not be otherwise. You don't look like a shopkeeper. I'll have thee made Captain Gilthead, and have thee march up and take in Pimlico, and have thee kill the bush at every tavern."

Pimlico was a resort town. "Take in" meant 1) capture as a soldier, and 2) tour as a tourist.

Tavern signs originally showed ivy plants, and so a tavern sign came to be known as a "bush." "To kill the bush" meant "to drink heavily."

Merecraft continued, "Thou shall have a wife if smocks will mount, boy."

Smocks can mount — that is, be lifted. The word "smock" also meant "woman," and women can mount men.

Merecraft turned to old Gilthead, the father, and asked, "What do you have? You have there now some Bristol-stone or Cornish counterfeit you'd put upon us?'

Fitzdottrel was in the market for a diamond ring, but Merecraft was asking Gilthead if he had brought a diamond substitute rather than a real diamond.

Gilthead showed him a jewel and said, "No, sir, I assure you that this is a real diamond. Look at its luster! The luster will speak for itself! I'll give you permission to put it in the mill for grinding."

Diamond substitutes were softer than real diamonds. Gilthead was saying that this was a real diamond that would survive grinding in a mill.

Gilthead continued, "It is not a great, large stone, but it is a true paragon of a diamond. This has all its corners — it has been perfectly cut. View it well."

"It's yellow," Merecraft said.

The color yellow indicated impurities in the diamond.

"Upon my faith, sir, it is of the right black luster, and very deep," Gilthead said. "It's set without a foil, too."

A foil is a thin sheet of metal placed under the diamond to show off its luster.

Gilthead displayed another jewel and said, "Here's one of the yellow luster that I'll sell cheap."

Merecraft said, "And what do you value this at? Thirty pounds?"

"No, sir," Gilthead said. "It cost me forty before it was set."

Forty what? Pounds? Something else?

"Turnings, you mean?" Merecraft said.

Turnings are actions that chip off the bad parts of the diamond.

Merecraft continued, "I know your equivocations. You're grown the better fathers of them lately."

He meant that Gilthead and other Jews had learned how to equivocate better than the Jesuit fathers.

He continued, "Well, where it must go, it will be judged, and therefore look that it is right. You shall have fifty pounds for it. Not a denier more!"

Earlier, Gilthead had talked to his son about Merecraft's summons: Gilthead would sell a ring for forty pounds that was not worth thirty pounds.

Merecraft then said to Fitzdottrel, "And because you would have things dispatched quickly, sir, I'll go immediately and find and talk to this Spanish lady. If you think it is good, sir, since you have a hundred pieces ready, you may part with those now, to serve my kinsman's turns, so that he may wait upon you at once the freer. And you will then take the hundred pieces when you have signed and sealed the agreement with Gilthead."

"I don't care if I do," Fitzdottrel said. "I agree."

"And dispatch all together," Merecraft said.

Fitzdottrel handed over the hundred pieces, saying, "There, they're exactly the right number: a hundred pieces! I have counted them twice a day for the past two months."

"Well, go and sign your agreement, sir, and then make your return here as speedily as you can."

He showed Fitzdottrel, Gilthead, and Plutarchus to the door, through which they exited.

Merecraft then began to split the money.

"Come, give it to me," Everill said.

"Quiet, sir —" Merecraft began.

"Indeed, and fair, too, then!" Everill said. "I'll permit no delaying in getting my share, sir."

"But you will listen to me?" Merecraft asked.

"Yes, when I have received my dividend," Everill said.

"There's forty pieces for you," Merecraft said.

"What is this for?" Everill said.

He expected more.

"It's your half," Merecraft said. "You know that Gilthead must have twenty pieces."

"And what about your ring there?" Everill said. "Shall I have none of that?"

"Oh, that's to be given to a lady," Merecraft said.

"Is that so?" Everill asked.

"By that good light, it is," Merecraft said.

"Come, give me ten pieces more, then," Everill said.

"Why?" Merecraft asked.

"Twenty pieces for Gilthead?" Everill said. "Sir, do you think I'll allow him to have any such share?"

"You must."

"Must I?" Everill said. "You do your musts, sir, and I'll do mine. You will not part with the whole, sir? Will you? Bull! Give me ten more pieces!"

"By what law do you do this?" Merecraft asked.

"Even lion-law, sir, or else I must roar."

Everill meant that unless he received more money he would tell people about Merecraft's cons.

"Good!" Merecraft said, meaning that Everill could yell and complain if he wanted to.

"You've heard how the ass made his divisions 'wisely'?" Everill asked.

An ass, a fox, and a lion made a partnership and went hunting. After they had killed prey, the ass divided the prey into three equal shares: one each for the ass, the fox, and the lion. The lion, however, was not happy with an equal share and so it killed the ass and added it to the slaughtered prey and asked the fox to divide the prey. The fox divided the prey into three equal shares and gave the lion two of the shares, making the lion happy so it would not kill the fox.

"And I am he, I thank you," Merecraft said.

He had equally and fairly divided the money.

"Much good may it do you, sir," Everill said, meaning that it would not do Merecraft any good.

He took ten extra pieces.

"I shall be rid of this tyranny one day!" Merecraft said.

"Not while you eat and lie about the town here, and cheat in your bullion-hose — your padded trousers," Everill said, "and not while I stand beside you and give you the benefit of my reputable name, and conduct your business, adjourn your beatings every term by postponing your trials in which you would face your creditors, and find new parties whom you can con with your projects."

Everill helped Merecraft in his cons by seeming to be a reputable man about town whom people could trust and then introducing them to Merecraft.

He continued, "I have now a pretty task of it, to hold you in with your Lady Tailbush. But the trick will be how we shall both come off without paying for what we will commit?"

"Leave off your doubting," Merecraft said, "and do your part — do what's assigned to you. I have never failed yet."

Everill said, "Give some credit to your aides, such as myself. You're always unthankful.

"Where shall I soon meet you? You have some feat to do alone now, I see. You wish me to leave. Well, I will find you out, and bring you afterward to the audit — the reckoning."

He exited.

"By God's light!" Merecraft said. "There's Engine's share, too. I had forgot!"

Engine should have received a share of the hundred pieces. So Merecraft, in fact, had *not* equally and fairly divided the money.

Merecraft continued, "This reign is too-too-unsupportable! I must relieve myself of this vassalage to Everill."

He heard a noise, looked up, and said, "Engine! Welcome."

Engine and Wittipol entered the room.

Merecraft took Engine aside and asked, "How goes the cry?"

The cry was a hunting cry. Merecraft was asking how the hunt for Dick Robinson was going.

Engine replied, "Excellently well!"

"Will it do?" Merecraft asked. "Where's Robinson?"

"Here is the gentleman, sir, who will undertake the role of the Spanish lady himself," Engine said. "I have acquainted him with the facts of the matter."

"Why did you do that?" Merecraft asked.

The fewer people who know about a con, the better.

"Why, Robinson would have told him — he's his friend — anyway, you know," Engine said. "And he's a pleasant wit; he will not hurt anything you purpose. Also, he's of the opinion that Robinson might lack the audacity to perform the part, the Spanish lady being such a gallant — such a fashionable lady. Now he has been in Spain, and knows the fashions there, and can discourse; and being but mirth, he says, leave it to his care — he can handle the part well."

"But he is too tall to play the Spanish lady!" Merecraft objected.

"As for that, he has the most splendid solution — you'll love him for it! He will say that he — that is, the Spanish lady — is wearing *cioppinos*, that is, soles worn under shoes to give extra height. And he will say that they do so in Spain. And Robinson is as tall as he is."

"Is that true?" Merecraft asked.

"Completely," Engine said.

"I had rather trust a gentleman with the part, of the two," Merecraft said.

Wittipol was a gentleman.

"I ask you to go to him then, sir, and greet him," Engine said.

They went over to Wittipol, and Merecraft said to him, "Sir, my friend Engine has acquainted you with a strange business here."

"A merry one, sir," Wittipol said. "The Duke of Drowned-land and his Duchess?"

"Yes, sir," Merecraft said. "Now that the conjurers have laid him by, I have made bold to borrow him a while —"

The conjurors were lying low because King James I had ordered that the laws against conjuring be enforced more rigorously. This gave con men such as Merecraft a chance to con Fitzdottrel.

"With the purpose still to put him out, I hope, to his best use?" Wittipol asked.

The conjurors and Merecraft believed that the best use of Fitzdottrel was to get as much money as possible from him. As of now, Wittipol had no objections.

"Yes, sir," Merecraft said.

"Don't worry about that small part that I am entrusted with," Wittipol said. "I would not miss out on doing it because of the mirth that will follow from it; and well, I have a fancy to do it."

His fancy was to get close to Fitzdottrel's wife.

"Sir, that will make it well," Merecraft said.

"You will say that it is so," Wittipol said.

He knew very well that Merecraft was a con man.

Wittipol then asked, "Where must I put on my costume so I can play the Spanish lady?"

"At my house, sir," Engine said.

"You shall have a guaranteed share, sir, in what Fitzdottrel yields to the sixpence," Merecraft said.

Wittipol did not want the money.

"You shall pardon me," he said. "I will share, sir, in your sports only; I am here for entertainment. I want nothing of your profits. But you must furnish me with the trappings of the Spanish lady: my coach, my *guarda-duennas* —"

Guarda-duennas are the Spanish lady's attendants.

"Engine's your *provedor*," Merecraft said.

Engine would provide those trappings.

Merecraft then said, "But sir, I must — now that I've entered trust with you thus far, and now that I have confidence in your quality — acquaint you with some additional information.

"The place designed to be the scene for this our merry matter, because it must have the support of women to draw conversation, and offer it, is nearby here, at the Lady Tailbush's."

Fitzdottrel and the Spanish lady would meet in a group of other people where conversation between the two could take place. A respectable woman would not meet privately a man to whom she was not married or related or who was not her trusted — and preferably elderly — servant. Of course, not all women are respectable, but even the women lacking respectability usually want to keep up appearances.

"I know her, sir," Wittipol said, "and her gentleman usher."

"You know Master Ambler?" Merecraft asked.

"Yes, sir," Wittipol answered.

"Sir, it shall be no shame to me to confess to you that we poor gentlemen who lack acres must for our needs turn fools up and plow ladies sometimes to try what glebe — quality of soil — they are; and this woman is no unfruitful piece. She and I now are on a project for the manufacture and selling of a new kind of fucus — makeup, for ladies — to benefit the kingdom, wherein she herself has travailed especially, by way of service to her sex, and hopes to get a monopoly for this product from King James I as the reward for her invention."

"What is her end in this?" Wittipol asked. "What is it she wants?"

"Merely ambition, sir, to grow great, and court it — act as a court lady — with those who have secrets, although she pretends to have some other more altruistic end.

"She's dealing already upon security for the shares, and Master Ambler has been named examiner for the ingredients and the register of what is sold, and he shall keep the office.

"Now, if she speaks confidentially with you about this — as I must make the leading thread to your becoming acquainted with her that your experience gotten through your being abroad will help our business — think of some pretty additions just to keep her floating, by which I mean just to keep her interested. It may be she will offer you a part. Any strange names of —"

"Sir, I have my instructions," Wittipol said. "Isn't it high time to be getting ready?"

Wittipol did not want to help Merecraft in his cons, although he was willing to play the Spanish lady in order to get close to Fitzdottrel's wife.

"Yes, sir," Merecraft said.

"The fool's in sight — Dottrel," Engine said, seeing Fitzdottrel coming.

"Leave, then," Merecraft said.

Wittipol and Engine exited.

Fitzdottrel entered the room.

"Returned so soon?" Merecraft said.

"Yes, here's the ring" — Fitzdottrel held it up — "I have signed for it and for the loan. But there's not so much gold in all the Goldsmith's Row in Cheapside, Gilthead says, until it comes from the Mint."

Fitzdottrel had given Merecraft a hundred pieces, and he was supposed to get a hundred pieces from Gilthead after signing for the ring and for the loan, but Gilthead had said that the hundred pieces were not available.

Fitzdottrel said, "The gold has been taken up for the gamblers."

"There's a shopkeeper's-trick!" Merecraft said. "A plague on them."

"He swears that it is true," Fitzdottrel said.

"He'll swear, and forswear, too," Merecraft said. "It is his trade. You should not have left him."

"By God's eyelid, I can go back and beat him, yet," Fitzdottrel said.

"No, now let him alone," Merecraft said.

"I was so earnest after the main business," Fitzdottrel said. "I wanted to get this ring and go."

"True, and it is time for the ring," Merecraft said. "I've learned, sir, since you went to see Gilthead, that Her Ladyship the Spanish lady will eat soon with the Lady Tailbush, who is close by here."

"In the lane here?" Fitzdottrel asked.

"Yes," Merecraft said. "If you have a servant now of good appearance, well dressed, and with a lively and voluble tongue, neither too big nor too little for his mouth, who could deliver your wife's compliment, to send along with —"

Fitzdottrel interrupted, "I have such a servant, sir, a very handsome, gentleman-like fellow, whom I intend to make my duchess' usher — I employed him just this morning, too. I'll call him to you. The worst thing about him is his name."

"She'll take no note of his name, just of his message," Merecraft said.

Fitzdottrel called, "Devil!"

Pug entered the room.

Fitzdottrel pointed to Pug and asked Merecraft, "How do you like him, sir?"

He said to Pug, "Walk around a little. Let's see you move."

Pug walked around a little.

"He'll serve, sir," Merecraft said. "Give the ring to him, and let him go along with me. I'll help to present him, and it."

Fitzdottrel gave Pug the ring and said, "Sirrah, look that you discharge this task well, if you expect to keep your job here. Do you hear, go on, acquit yourself with all honors."

He said to Merecraft, "I would like to see him do it."

He would like to see Pug meet the Spanish lady and give the ring to her.

"Trust him with it," Merecraft said.

Fitzdottrel gave Pug some instructions: "Remember kissing of your hand, and answering with the French-time, in flexure of your body."

Kissing one's own hand was part of the courtly etiquette of the time. The French-time was a fancy low bow.

He continued, "I could now so instruct him! And for his words —"

Merecraft interrupted, "I'll put them in his mouth."

"Oh, but I have learned the words from the very academies," Fitzdottrel said.

"Sir, you'll have use for them yourself soon, I promise you, after dinner, when you are called," Merecraft said.

"By God's light, that'll be just play-time," Fitzdottrel said. "It cannot be! I must not miss the play!"

Many people customarily ate dinner at midday, which was sometimes followed by seeing a play that began at 3 p.m.

"Sir, but you must go to the Spanish lady, if she wants to sit and talk after dinner," Merecraft said. "She's the president."

"By God's eyelid, the play is *The Devil*!" Fitzdottrel said.

He really wanted to see the play — or at least part of it — because it had a devil in it.

"Even if it were *The Devil and His Dam*, too, you must now apply yourself, sir, to this wholly, or lose all," Merecraft said.

Fitzdottrel began, "If I could but see a part of the play —"

"Sir, don't even think about doing it," Merecraft said.

"If I could see only one act, I would not care — I want only to be seen to rise, and to go away, in order to vex the actors, and to punish their playwright — and keep him in awe!" Fitzdottrel said.

"But what if he is one who will not be awed, but will instead laugh at you?" Merecraft asked. "What then?"

"Then he shall pay for his dinner himself," Fitzdottrel said.

Audience members often treated playwrights to a late dinner.

"Perhaps he would do that twice rather than thank you," Merecraft said. "Come, get *The Devil* out of your head, my lord — I'll call you so in private still — and remember this: You were, sweet lord, talking about bringing a business to the Office of Dependency."

"Yes," Fitzdottrel said.

"Why shouldn't you, sir, carry it on yourself, before the Office of Dependency be up and running? You would show the world that you had no need of any man's direction, in point, sir, of sufficiency? I speak against a kinsman, but I speak as one who tenders Your Grace's good."

He was speaking against a kinsman because, supposedly, he was taking business away from Everill.

"I thank you," Fitzdottrel said. "To proceed —"

Merecraft interrupted, "To publications. Have your deed drawn up immediately, and leave a blank to put in your beneficiaries: one, two, or more, as you see cause —"

Merecraft was hoping to have his name put in the deed as a beneficiary: He wanted to take control of Fitzdottrel's estate.

"I thank you heartily, I do thank you," Fitzdottrel said. "Not a word more, I ask you, as you love and respect me. Let me alone."

He was angry with himself and thought, *That I could not think of this as well as he! Oh, I could beat my infinite blockhead! I should have thought of doing that!*

He exited.

Merecraft said to Pug, "Come, we must go this way."

They began walking to the building where Lady Tailbush lived.

"How far is it?" Pug asked.

"Close by here over the way," Merecraft said.

He thought, *Now, I need to gain possession of this ring from this same fellow, Fitzdottrel's servant. I need to secure the ring before he gives it to the Spanish lady.*

Pug asked, "Sir, are the ladies we are going to see pretty and splendidly dressed?"

"Oh, yes," Merecraft said.

"And shall I see them, and speak to them?" Pug asked.

"What else?" Merecraft answered.

Trains arrived, carrying a cloak and bag.

Merecraft privately asked him, "Do you have your false beard with you, Trains?"

"Yes," Trains replied.

"And is this one of your double cloaks?" Merecraft asked.

A double cloak was a reversible cloak that had two sides in different colors and styles, making a quick change in appearance easy when it was needed.

"It is the best of them," Trains said.

"Be ready then," Merecraft said.

Trains exited.

Seeing Pitfall coming, Merecraft greeted her: "Sweet Pitfall!"

— 3.6 —

Pitfall, who was Lady Tailbush's female attendant, entered the scene.

Merecraft said to her, "Come, I must kiss —"

He attempted to kiss her, but she said, "Get away from me!"

"I'll set thee up again," Merecraft said. "Never fear that. Can thou never get a bird? No thrushes hungry? Stay until cold weather comes, and I'll help thee to an ouzel or a fieldfare."

Merecraft would set Pitfall up again after she had trapped a bird. In this society, one meaning of "bird" was "young woman," but a few years earlier, another meaning was "young man." Quite possibly, Pitfall made extra money by having sex with young men. Merecraft would set her up again after a session in bed.

A pitfall is a trap; in this society, it is especially a trap for birds. Ouzels and fieldfares are kinds of birds that arrive in England in the autumn, when the weather gets colder.

Merecraft asked her, "Who's within, with Madam Tailbush?"

"I'll tell you straightaway," she said.

She quickly went inside the building where Lady Tailbush lived.

Merecraft said to Pug, "Please stay here a while, sir. I'll go in."

He went inside.

Pug, who had heard enough to guess that Pitfall was a prostitute, at least part-time, said to himself, "I do so long to have a little lechery, while I am in this body! I would taste of every sin a little, if it might be after the manner of man!"

Pitfall returned, and Pug said to her, "Sweetheart!"

"What do you want, sir?" Pitfall said.

"Nothing but to fall into you," Pug said.

He, or a certain part of his body, would like to fall into her "pit."

He continued, "I want to be your blackbird, my pretty pit. As the gentleman said, I want to be your song thrush. I want to lie tame and taken with you."

One meaning of the word "taken" is "captured." One meaning of "taken with" is "attracted by or charmed by."

99

He continued, "Here is gold! Use it to buy yourself so much new dress material from the shop — as long as I may take the old dress up —"

He wanted to pay her to allow him to lift her old dress up for sex.

Trains, wearing a false beard and the other side of his reversible cloak, arrived and using a disguised voice said to Pug, "Sir, you must send the gentleman the ring."

Intent on having sex with Pitfall and so not paying enough attention to the disguised Trains, Pug handed over the ring and said, "There it is."

The disguised Trains exited with the ring.

Pug said to Pitfall, "Look, will you be foolish, Pit?"

He meant: Would you like to fool around?

"This is strange rudeness," Pitfall said.

Pug began, "Dear Pit —"

Pitfall interrupted, "I'll call for help, I swear!"

She quickly exited.

Merecraft returned and said to Pug, "Where are you, sir? Is your ring ready? Go with me."

"I sent the ring to you," Pug said.

Acting surprised, Merecraft said, "To me? When? By whom?"

"A fellow was here, just now," Pug said. "He came for it in your name."

"I sent no one for the ring, to be sure," Merecraft said. "My intention was always that you should deliver it to the Spanish lady yourself. That was your master's order to you, you know. What fellow was it? Do you know him?"

"Here, just now, he got it!" Pug said.

Trains returned, wearing the other side of the reversible cloak and no longer wearing a false beard as a disguise.

"Have you seen anyone, Trains?" Merecraft asked.

"No, not I," Trains replied.

"The gentlewoman saw him," Pug said, referring to Pitfall.

"Ask her about it," Merecraft ordered Trains.

Trains exited.

Pug said to himself, "I was so focused upon Pitfall that I paid no attention to the man! My devilish chief has put me here in flesh to shame me! I perceive nothing with this dull body I am in! I attempt nothing that will succeed!"

Trains returned and said, "Sir, she saw no one, she says."

Pug said to himself, "Satan himself has taken a shape and disguise to abuse me. It could not be otherwise!"

"This is more than strange, that you should be so reckless!" Merecraft said to Pug. "What'll you do, sir? How will you answer when you are questioned about this?"

Pug said to himself, "I would run away from my flesh if I could; I would take off this body of mankind. This is such a scorn! And it will be a new exercise for my archduke — Satan! He will get exercise by punishing me! Woe to the several cudgels that must suffer on this back of mine!"

He asked Merecraft, "Do you know of anything that might help me, sir?"

"Alas!" Merecraft said. "The need for help is so immediate."

"I ask, sir, credit for another ring, only until tomorrow!" Pug said.

Pug would be back in Hell tomorrow.

"There is not enough time to get another ring, sir," Merecraft said. "But, however, the lady is a noble lady, and will, to save a gentleman from rebuke, be entreated to say that she has received the ring."

"Do you think so?" Pug asked. "Will she agree to say that she has received the ring?"

"No doubt, for such a reason," Merecraft said. "It will be a lady's bravery and her pride. She will take pride in doing a good deed."

"And not let the good deed be known later in case Fitzdottrel learns about it?" Pug asked.

"That would be treacherous!" Merecraft said. "Upon my word, be confident.

"Tell this to your master: My lady president — the Spanish lady — sits this afternoon and will receive guests. She has accepted the gift of the ring, and she commends her services to your lady duchess: Mrs. Frances Dotterel.

"You may say that she's a civil lady, and she gives to your lady duchess all her respects already. She also wants you to tell her that she lives but to receive her wished commandments and have the honor here to kiss her hands, for which reason she'll stay here for yet another hour.

"Hasten to your prince. Leave!"

Doubtful, Pug asked, "And, sir, you will take care that the excuse is perfect?"

"You confess your fears too much," Merecraft said.

"I am more worried about the shame," Pug said.

He would be shamed in Hell for having fallen victim to a con.

"I'll rid you of either," Merecraft said.

But not rid Pug of both fear of Fitzdottrel and shame by Satan?

CHAPTER 4

— 4.1 —

In her home, Lady Tailbush and Merecraft talked about the project they were working on together.

"A pox upon referring the project to commissioners!" Lady Tailbush said. "I'd rather hear that it were past the seals."

To get the monopoly, projects were submitted to commissioners who would recommend that some projects be granted a monopoly. If the recommendation were accepted, the monopoly would be granted with a document bearing the privy seal.

To get a project submitted to the commissioners, various courtiers were used. Some courtiers were more effective than others.

"Your courtiers move so snail-like in your business," Lady Tailbush complained. "I wish I had not begun to do business with you."

"We must move, madam, in order, by degrees," Merecraft replied. "We must not jump."

"Why, there was Sir John Moneyman — he could jump a business quickly," she replied.

"True, he had great friends," Merecraft said. "But although some, sweet madam, can leap ditches, we must not all shun going over bridges. The harder parts, I reckon, are done. Now the project has been referred to the commissioners."

He then flattered her: "You are infinitely bound to the ladies — they have so sung the praises of your new brand of makeup."

"Do they like it, then? " Lady Tailbush asked.

"They have sent the Spanish lady to congratulate you."

"I must send them thanks, and some remembrances," Lady Tailbush said.

"That you must, and you must visit them," Merecraft said. "Where's Ambler?"

"Lost," Lady Tailbush said. "Today we cannot hear of him."

"We cannot, madam?" Merecraft asked.

"No, in good faith," Lady Tailbush said. "They say he did not sleep at home last night. And here has fallen a business between your cousin and Master Manly that has disquieted us all."

"So I hear, madam," Merecraft said. "Please tell me, what happened?"

"Truly, it appears completely ill on your kinsman Everill's part," Lady Tailbush said. "You may have heard that Manly is a suitor to me, I am sure —"

"I guessed it, madam," Merecraft said.

"And it seems he entrusted your cousin Everill to let fall some fair reports of him to me," Lady Tailbush said. "Manly wanted Everill to talk him up to me."

"Which he did," Merecraft said.

"Which he did not," Lady Tailbush said. "So far from it, as Manly learned when he came in and heard Everill saying bad things about him."

"What!" Merecraft said. "And what did Manly say to him?"

"Enough, I assure you," Lady Tailbush said, "and with such scorn of him and the injury he did that I wonder how Everill bore it — but that guilt undoes many men's valors."

Many behind-the-back slanderers lack courage.

Manly entered the room.

Merecraft said, "Here comes Manly."

Preparing to leave, Manly said to Lady Tailbush, "Madam, I'll take my leave —"

"You shall not go, truly," Lady Tailbush said. "I'll have you stay and see this Spanish miracle of our English lady."

The Spanish lady, of course, was supposed to be an English lady who dressed in Spanish clothing.

"Let me ask Your Ladyship to lay your commands on me some other time," Manly said.

"Now, I protest," Lady Tailbush said, "and I will have all pieced together, and all made friends again."

"It will be but ill soldered," Manly said.

He and Everill could not be friends although possibly they might be civil to each other.

"You are too much affected by it," Lady Tailbush said.

"I cannot, Madam, but think about it because of the injustice," Manly said.

"Sir, his kinsman — Merecraft — here is sorry," Lady Tailbush said.

Merecraft said, "Not I, madam, I am no kin to him — we just call each other cousins."

He then said to Manly, "And even if we really were cousins, sir, I have no relation to his crimes."

The word "crime" also meant "sin."

"You are not charged with his crimes," Manly said. "I can accuse, sir, none but my own judgment, for although it were his crime so to betray me, I'm sure it was more my own at all to trust him. But he therein used his old manners, and his savor was strongly what he was before."

"His old tricks" consisted of unethical behaviors, and his savor was that of a stink.

"Come, he will change!" Lady Tailbush said.

"Indeed, I must never think that he will change," Manly said. "Nor would it be reasonable of me to expect that for my sake he should put off a nature he sucked in with his milk."

Everill had been bad since he was a baby, according to Manly. It was his nature. He had sucked evil into him while sucking his mother's milk.

Of course, Manly was also criticizing Everill's mother.

Manly continued, "It may be, madam, deceiving trust is all he has to trust to. If so, I shall be loath that any hope of mine should take away his means of making a living."

Yes, Everill's sole means of making a living was by deceiving those who trusted him: He was a con man.

"You're sharp, sir," Lady Tailbush said.

Manly was sharp in his criticism of Everill. Although Lady Tailbush did not mean to say it, he was also intelligent in his criticism of Everill.

Yet Manly was tolerant of bad behavior in others. He did not attempt to get his friend Wittipol to not try to seduce another man's wife, and he said openly now that he did not want to take away Everill's way of making a living, even if that way were unethical. He was a forgiving — perhaps, or definitely, too forgiving — man.

Lady Tailbush added, "This act may make him honest."

The act was being reconciled with Manly.

Manly replied, "If he were to be made honest by an act of Parliament, I would not alter in my lack of faith in him."

Seeing Lady Eitherside enter the room, Lady Tailbush said, "Eitherside! Welcome, dear Eitherside! How are you, good wench? Thou have been a stranger! I have not seen thee all this week."

Manly and Merecraft began to talk together quietly.

"I am always your servant, madam," Lady Eitherside said.

"Where have thou been?" Lady Tailbush said. "I did so long to see thee."

"Visiting, and I am so tired!" Lady Eitherside said. "I protest, madam, visiting is a monstrous trouble."

Engaging in social activities such as visiting others can be exhausting, but many people who actually enjoy visiting complain about visiting.

"And so it is," Lady Tailbush said. "I swear I must begin my visits tomorrow — I wish that they were over — at court. It tortures me to think about them."

"I hear you have a reason for your visits, madam," Lady Eitherside said. "Your suit goes on."

The suit was to get a monopoly for the production of the new makeup.

"Who told thee?" Lady Tailbush asked.

"One who can tell: Master Eitherside."

"Oh, thy husband," Lady Tailbush said, "Yes, indeed, there's life in it now; the suit has been referred to the commissioners. If we once see it receive the Privy Seal and the monopoly, wench, then we can compete with the rich set. We'll have the great coach, six horses, and the two coachmen, with my Ambler bareheaded, and my three women-servants; we will live, truly, as the examples of the town, and govern it. I'll lead the fashion always."

"You do that now, sweet madam," Lady Eitherside said.

"Oh, but then I'll every day bring up some new project," Lady Tailbush said. "Thou and I, Eitherside, will first be in it; I will give it thee, and they shall follow us. Thou shall, I swear, wear every month a new gown out of it."

"Thank you, good madam."

"I ask thee to call me Tailbush, as I call thee Eitherside," Lady Tailbush said. "I don't love this 'madam.'"

Lady Tailbush had greater social status than Lady Eitherside, who used the respectful "you" when talking to her. Lady Tailbush used "thou" and "thee" when talking to Lady Eitherside.

"Then I protest to you, Tailbush, that I am glad your business so succeeds," Lady Eitherside said.

"I thank thee, good Eitherside," Lady Tailbush said.

"But Master Eitherside tells me that he likes your other business better."

"Which business is that?" Lady Tailbush asked.

"The business of the toothpicks," Lady Eitherside said.

"I have never heard about it," Lady Tailbush said.

"Ask Master Merecraft about it," Lady Eitherside said.

Merecraft, who was still talking quietly with Manly, overheard and said, "Madam?"

He then said to Manly about Everill, "He's one — in a word, I'll trust his malice with any man's credit I would have abused."

Merecraft was saying that he could count on Everill to undermine another man's reputation — Everill could be counted on to slander another man.

"Sir, if you think you please me in this, you are deceived," Manly said.

"No," Merecraft said, "but because my lady named him as my kinsman, I want to let you know what I think about him, and I ask you to judge me by my opinion of him!"

"So I do," Manly said. "Ill men's friends are as unfaithful as themselves."

Ill men speak ill about others, and Manly was saying that judging by Merecraft's words, the friends of ill men also spoke ill about others.

"Do you hear me?" Lady Tailbush asked Merecraft. "Do you have a business about toothpicks?"

"Yes, madam," Merecraft said. "Didn't I ever tell you about it? I meant to have offered it to Your Ladyship once the patent was perfected."

"What is it?" Lady Tailbush asked.

"The business is for serving the whole state with toothpicks," Merecraft said. "It's somewhat an intricate business to discourse, but I show how much the subject is abused, first, in that one commodity: The toothpicks are badly made. Then I show what diseases and putrefactions in the gums those toothpicks that are made of adulterated and false wood breed!

"My plot for reformation of these abuses is as follows:

"To have all toothpicks brought to an office, there to receive a seal of approval.

"Such people who counterfeit the toothpicks and make bad ones, however, shall be fined.

"And last, for selling them, to have a book printed to teach their proper use, which every child who can read shall have throughout the kingdom. By reading the book, they will learn how to properly pick their teeth.

"Beginning early to practice the proper procedure of picking, and practicing some other rules, such as never sleeping with the mouth open, and chewing some gum, will preserve the breath and make it pure, and so free from taint —"

Seeing Trains arrive, Merecraft stopped and asked him, "What do you have to tell me?"

Trains whispered to him.

"In good faith, it sounds like a very pretty business!" Lady Tailbush said.

"So Master Eitherside says, madam," Lady Eitherside said.

Merecraft said, "The Spanish lady has come."

"Has she?" Lady Tailbush said. "Good, show her in."

Merecraft exited.

"My Ambler was never so unfortunately absent," Lady Tailbush said. "Eitherside, how do I look today? Am I not dressed smartly?"

She looked in her mirror.

"Yes, you are, truly, madam," Lady Eitherside said.

"A pox on the word 'madam'!" Lady Tailbush said. "Won't you stop saying that?"

"Yes, good Tailbush," Lady Eitherside said.

"So? Doesn't that sound better?" Lady Tailbush asked.

She then asked, "What vile fucus — makeup — is this thou have got on?"

"It is pearl," Lady Eitherside said.

"Pearl?" Lady Tailbush said. "Oyster shells! As I breathe, Eitherside, I know it.

"Here comes, they say, a wonder, sirrah, who has been in Spain, and who will teach us all. She's been sent to me from court to congratulate me. Please, let's observe her and see what faults she has, so that we may laugh at them when she has gone."

"That we will heartily, Tailbush," Lady Eitherside said.

"Oh, me!" Lady Tailbush said, seeing Wittipol dressed as the Spanish lady. "She is the very infanta of the giants!"

An "infanta" is a daughter of a Spanish noble family, but the word was also used to describe a woman, particularly one of pompous display.

Wittipol was tall to begin with, but he was also wearing *cioppinos*.

Merecraft and Wittipol, who was dressed as the Spanish lady, walked over to Lady Tailbush.

Merecraft said to Lady Tailbush, "Here is a noble lady, madam, come from your great friends at court to see Your Ladyship and have the honor of your acquaintance.

"Sir, she does us honor," Lady Tailbush said.

To help preserve his disguise, Wittipol (the Spanish lady) said to Merecraft, "Please, say to Her Ladyship that it is the manner of Spain to embrace only, and never to kiss. She will excuse the custom!"

"Your use of it is law," Lady Tailbush said. "If it pleases you, sweet madam, take a seat."

"Yes, madam," Wittipol (the Spanish lady) said. "I have had the favor, through a world of fair reporting about you, to know your virtues, madam, and in that name have desired the happiness of presenting my service to Your Ladyship."

"Your love, madam — not your service!" Lady Tailbush said. "Otherwise, I cannot accept it."

"Both my service and my love for you are due, madam, to your great undertakings," Wittipol (the Spanish lady) said.

"Great?" Lady Tailbush said. "Truly, madam, they are my friends who think my undertakings to be anything. If I can do my sex any service by my undertakings, I've achieved my aims, madam."

"And they are noble ones, which make a multitude beholden to you, madam," Wittipol (the Spanish lady) said. "The commonwealth of ladies must acknowledge you."

"Except some who are envious and malicious, madam," Lady Tailbush said.

"You're right in that, madam," Wittipol (the Spanish lady) said. "Some of that race I encountered just recently, who, it seems, have worked to find reasons to discredit your business."

"Who, sweet madam?" Lady Tailbush asked.

"Nay, the parties will not be worth your pause — they are most ruinous things, madam, that have put off all hope of being recovered to a degree of attractiveness and decency," Wittipol (the Spanish lady) said.

"But what are their reasons, madam?" Lady Tailbush said. "I would like to hear what they are."

"Some, madam, I remember," Wittipol (the Spanish lady) said. "They say that painting — using makeup — quite destroys the face —"

"Oh, that's an old criticism, madam," Lady Tailbush said.

"There are new ones, too," Wittipol (the Spanish lady) said. "They say that makeup corrupts the breath. They say that makeup has left so little sweetness in kissing that kissing is now used only for fashion, and shortly will be taken for a punishment. They say that makeup decays the front teeth that should guard the tongue and keep it from saying bad things — because of the use of makeup, the front teeth decay and from the mouth come words that run everlasting riot. And — which is worse — they say that because of makeup some ladies when they meet cannot be merry and laugh but instead they spit in one another's faces!"

Manly looked closely at the Spanish lady and began to recognize Wittipol.

Manley thought, *I should know this voice, and I should know this face, too.*

Wittipol (the Spanish lady) said, "Then they say that makeup is dangerous to all the fallen yet well-disposed mad-dames who are industrious and desire to earn their living with their sweat. For any distemper of heat and motion may displace the colors, and if the paint once runs about their faces, twenty to one, they will appear so ill-favored and ugly that their servants will run away, too, and leave the pleasure imperfect, and the reckoning also unpaid."

These "mad-dames" were madams and/or prostitutes. When their makeup ran, they looked ugly and lost all their "servants" — their lovers, aka customers, who left and did not pay.

"Pox, these are poets' reasons!" Lady Eitherside said.

"Some old lady who keeps a poet has devised these scandals," Lady Tailbush said.

"Truly, we must have the poets banished, madam, as Master Eitherside says," Lady Eitherside said.

One person who wanted the poets banished was Plato, or so one of his books advocated. In Plato's *Republic*, poets were banished for lying about the gods. Poets such as Homer showed the gods to be far from benevolent to human beings. According to Homer's *Iliad*, the gods were often petty.

Trains entered and whispered to Merecraft.

"Master Fitzdottrel!" Merecraft said. "And his wife! Where?"

He said to Wittipol (the Spanish lady), "Madam, the Duke of Drowned-land, who will be shortly, has arrived."

Wittipol (the Spanish lady) asked, "Is this my lord?"

"The same," Merecraft said.

Fitzdottrel, Mrs. Frances Fitzdottrel, and Pug walked over to them.

"I am your servant, madam," Fitzdottrel said.

Wittipol whispered to Manly, "How are you now, friend? Offended that I have found your haunt here?"

Manly whispered back, "No, but I am wondering at your strangely dressed venture here."

"My purpose is to show you what they are whom you so pursue," Wittipol whispered.

He intended to say things that would encourage Lady Tailbush, whom Manly was pursuing, and her friends to expose themselves as bad people.

Manly, who disliked Everill and Merecraft — two friends or associates of Lady Tailbush — whispered back, "I think it will prove a medicine against marriage to know their manners."

"Stay and profit, then," Wittipol whispered.

Merecraft said to Wittipol (the Spanish lady), "This is the lady, madam, whose prince has brought her here to be instructed."

Supposedly, she would be instructed in the manners of a higher social class than her and her husband's.

Merecraft presented Mrs. Frances Fitzdottrel to Wittipol (the Spanish lady).

"Will it please you to sit with us, lady?" Wittipol (the Spanish lady) asked.

Referring to Wittipol (the Spanish lady), Merecraft said to Fitzdottrel, "That's the lady-president."

"She is a goodly woman!" Fitzdottrel said.

"Goodly" meant both 1) good-looking and 2) large.

"I cannot see the ring, though," Fitzdottrel added.

"Sir, she has it," Merecraft said.

Continuing her earlier conversation with Wittipol (the Spanish lady), Lady Tailbush said, "But, madam, these are very feeble reasons for being against the use of makeup."

Wittipol (the Spanish lady) replied, "Therefore, I urged, madam, that the new complexion now to come forth in the name of Your Ladyship's fucus had no ingredient —"

"— but those I dare to eat, I assure you," Lady Tailbush interrupted.

"So do they in Spain," Wittipol (the Spanish lady) said.

"Sweet madam, be so liberal to give us the ingredients of some of your Spanish fucuses," Lady Tailbush said.

"They are infinite, madam," Wittipol (the Spanish lady) said.

Many ingredients were used in Spanish makeup.

"So I hear," Lady Tailbush said.

Wittipol (the Spanish lady) began to list the many ingredients. Lady Tailbush knew what some of them were and pretended to know what the others were. Readers are advised to do the same.

Wittipol (the Spanish lady) said, "They have water of gourds, water of radish, the white beans, flowers of glass [powdered glass], powdered thistles, rosmarine [rosemary], raw honey, mustard-seed, and improperly baked doughy bread, the crumbs of bread, goat's milk, and whites of eggs, camphor, and lily roots, the fat of swans, marrow of veal, white pigeons, and pine-kernels, the seeds of nettles, purslane [a kind of herb], and hare's gall, lemons, thin-skinned —"

Lady Eitherside interrupted, "How Her Ladyship has studied all excellent things!"

Wittipol (the Spanish lady) said, "These are only ordinary ingredients, madam. No, the true rarities are the *alvagada* [white lead] and *argentata* [white ceruse] of Queen Isabella!"

"Yes, what are their ingredients, gentle madam?" Lady Tailbush asked.

Wittipol (the Spanish lady) said, "Your *allum scagliola* [flaked gypsum], or *pol di pedra* [rock alum], and *zuccarino* [sugar paste]; turpentine of Abezzo [pitch-pine sap], washed in nine waters; *soda di levanter* [sodium carbonate], or your fern ashes; *benjamin di gotta* [a tree resin], *grasso di serpe* [snake's fat], *porcelletto marino* [sturgeon]; oils of *lentisco* [mastic gum], *zucche* [turnip], *mugia* [a kind of fish] make the admirable varnish for the face and give the right luster; but two drops rubbed on with a piece of scarlet make a lady of sixty look at sixteen. But, above all, the water of the white hen, of the Lady Estifania's!"

"Oh, yes, that same, good madam, I have heard of," Lady Tailbush said. "How is it done?"

Wittipol (the Spanish lady) replied, "Madam, you take your hen, pluck it, and skin it, and cleanse it of the innards. Then chop it, bones and all; add to four ounces of *carravicins*, *pipitas*, soap of Cyprus, make the decoction, and strain it. Then distill it, and keep it in your galley-pot [apothecary's jar] well sealed. Three drops will preserve skin from wrinkles, warts, spots, moles, blemish, or sun-burnings, and keep the skin *in decimo sexto*, forever bright and smooth as any mirror; and indeed, it is called the virgin's milk for the face, *oglio reale*. A ceruse that neither cold nor heat will hurt, when mixed with oil of myrrh, the red gillyflower called *cataputia*, and flowers of *rovistico* makes the best *muta*, or dye, of the whole world."

Wittipol, of course, was satirizing the making of beauty products. Keeping "the skin *in decimo sexton*" sounds as if the beauty product would keep the skin looking like that of a 16-year-old girl, but *in decimo sexton* actually refers to a small book whose leaves are each one-sixteenth of a full sheet of paper.

"Dear madam, will you let us be familiar?" Lady Tailbush asked. "Shall we be friends?"

Wittipol (the Spanish lady) replied, "I am Your Ladyship's servant."

Merecraft asked Fitzdottrel, "How do you like her?"

"She is admirable!" Fitzdottrel said. "But still I cannot see the ring."

He was mistrustful about his ring.

Ready to confess that he had been conned out of the ring, Pug said, "Sir!"

Hearing Pug, Merecraft said to himself, "I must deliver the ring, or everything will be ruined. This fool Fitzdottrel is so mistrustful."

He said to Wittipol (the Spanish lady), "Madam —"

He surreptitiously handed over the ring and whispered, "Sir, wear this ring, and please know that it was sent to you by Fitzdottrel's wife. And be sure to give her thanks."

He then whispered to Pug, "Don't dwindle, sir. Bear up."

"I thank you, sir," Pug, who had witnessed the handing over of the ring, said.

"But for the manner of Spain!" Lady Tailbush said. "Sweet madam, let us be bold, now we are friends. Are all the ladies there in the fashion?"

"None but grandees, madam, of the clasped train, which may be worn at length, too, or like this, upon my arm," Wittipol (the Spanish lady) said.

"And do they all wear *cioppinos*?" Lady Tailbush asked.

Cioppinos were soles that were worn under shoes to add height.

"Yes, if they are dressed in *punto*, madam," Wittipol (the Spanish lady) said.

"In *punto*" meant "in their best."

"Gilt as those are, madam?" Lady Tailbush asked.

Wittipol (the Spanish lady), who was wearing golden soles, replied, "Of goldsmith's work, madam, and set with diamonds; and their Spanish pumps of perfumed leather."

"Pumps" are shoes.

"I should think it hard to walk in them, madam," Lady Tailbush said.

"At first it is, madam," Wittipol (the Spanish lady) said.

"Do you ever fall in them?" Lady Tailbush asked.

"Never," Wittipol (the Spanish lady) replied.

"I swear, I should fall six times an hour!" Lady Eitherside said.

"But you have men at hand always to help you if you fall?" Lady Tailbush said.

"Only one, madam — the *guarda-duennas*, who is such a little old man as this man is," Wittipol (the Spanish lady) said, pointing to Trains.

"Alas!" Lady Eitherside said. "He can do nothing! This man!"

"Let me tell you, madam," Wittipol (the Spanish lady) said. "I saw in the court of Spain once a lady fall in the King's sight. She was stretched out on the ground, and there she lay, flat spread as an umbrella, with the hoop of her petticoat cracked here." — He pointed to a place on the hoop of the petticoat he was wearing. — "No man dared reach out a hand to help her, till the *guarda-duennas* came. A *guarda-duenna* is the only person allowed to touch a lady there; and he only by this finger."

"Haven't they any servants, madam, there?" Lady Eitherside asked. "Haven't they any friends?"

"An *escudero* or so, madam, who waits upon them in another coach, at a distance, and when they walk, or dance, nearby holds a handkerchief, and never presumes to touch them," Wittipol (the Spanish lady) said.

An *escudero* is a Spanish squire.

"This is scurvy!" Lady Eitherside said. "And a forced gravity — an unnatural formality! I do not like it. I like our own much better."

"It is more French and courtly, ours," Lady Tailbush said.

"And tastes more of liberty," Lady Eitherside said. "We may have our dozen of visitors at once make love to us."

This kind of making love was flirting — mostly. Perhaps.

"And in front of our husbands!" Lady Tailbush said.

"Husband?" Lady Eitherside said. "As I am honest, Tailbush, I think that if nobody should love me but my poor husband, I would just hang myself."

"Fortune forbid, wench, that so fair a neck should have so foul a necklace as a noose!" Lady Tailbush said.

"What I said is true, as I am handsome!" Lady Eitherside said.

Wittipol (the Spanish lady) said to Mrs. Frances Fitzdottrel, "I received, lady, a token from you, which I would not be so rude as to refuse, it being your first remembrance — gift to remember you by — to me."

Seeing the ring, Fitzdottrel whispered to Merecraft, "Oh, I am satisfied now!"

Merecraft whispered back, "Do you see the ring, sir?"

"But since you come to know me nearer and better, lady, I'll beg the honor that you will wear it for me," Wittipol (the Spanish lady) said. "It must be so."

Wittipol (the Spanish lady) gave the ring to Mrs. Frances Fitzdottrel.

Mrs. Frances Fitzdottrel said to herself, "Surely I have heard this voice before."

Merecraft whispered to Wittipol (the Spanish lady), "What are you doing, sir?"

"Would you have me be mercenary?" Wittipol (the Spanish lady) said. "We'll recompense it soon, in something else."

He meant that Merecraft would soon be able to get money from Fitzdottrel in some other way.

Merecraft and Trains exited.

"I do not love to be gulled, even in a trifling matter," Fitzdottrel said, satisfied now that he saw the ring. "Wife, do you hear? You're come into the school, wife, where you may learn — I know — anything! How to be fine, or fair, or great, or proud, or whatever you want, indeed, wife; here it is taught.

And I am glad that you may not say, another day, when honors come upon you, you lacked means."

He then let his wife know about his costs: "I have done my parts. Today I have been at fifty pounds charge, first, for a ring to get you entered here where you can learn the manners of this social class. Then I left my new play to wait upon you here, to see your entry into this society confirmed, so that I may say, both to my own eyes and ears — senses, you are my witness — she has enjoyed all helps that could be had, for love, or money —"

Mrs. Frances Fitzdottrel finished the sentence for him: "— to make a fool of her."

"Wife, that's your malice, the wickedness of your nature to interpret your husband's kindness thus," Fitzdottrel said. "But I'll not stop trying always to do good despite your depraved disposition. Take note of it. Bend this stubborn will of yours; be great in society."

Lady Tailbush asked Wittipol (the Spanish lady), "Good madam, whom do the Spanish grandees use in carrying messages?"

"They commonly use their slaves, madam," Wittipol (the Spanish lady) said.

"And does Your Ladyship think that so good, madam?" Lady Tailbush asked.

"No, indeed, madam," Wittipol (the Spanish lady) said. "In such matters I prefer the fashion of England by far. I prefer the use of your young delicate page, or discreet usher, to carry messages."

"And I go with Your Ladyship in opinion directly for your gentleman-usher," Fitzdottrel said. "There's not a finer officer who goes on ground."

"If he is made and broken in to his place, once," Wittipol (the Spanish lady) said.

"I presuppose him to be so," Fitzdottrel said.

"And they are fitter managers, too, sir, but I would have them called our *escuderos*," Wittipol (the Spanish lady) said.

"Good," Fitzdottrel said.

"Let's say that I would send to Your Ladyship who, I presume, has gathered all the dear secrets to know how to make *pastillos* of the Duchess of Braganza, *coquettas, almojavanas, mantecadas, alcorças, mustaccioli,*" Wittipol (the Spanish lady) said.

All of the foreign words were for various kinds of sweets.

Wittipol (the Spanish lady) continued, "Or say it were the *peladore* [depilatory] of Isabella, or balls [pills] against the itch, or *aqua nanfa* [orange water], or oil of jessamine [jasmine] for gloves of the Marquess Muja. Or for the head, and hair; why, these are offices —"

Fitzdottrel interrupted, "— fit for a gentleman, not a slave."

Wittipol (the Spanish lady) said, "They only might ask for your *piveti*, aka Spanish coal, an aromatic substance, to burn, and sweeten a room; but the arcane secrets of ladies' cabinets —"

Fitzdottrel interrupted, "— should be elsewhere trusted."

He then said to Wittipol (the Spanish lady), "You're much about the truth — you're absolutely right."

He then said, "Sweet honored ladies, let me fall in with you."

He walked into the midst of the ladies and said, "I have my female wit, as well as my male wit. And I know what suits a lady of spirit, or a woman of fashion!"

By saying that he had "my female wit, as well as my male wit," Fitzdottrel was identifying himself as a womanish man, something that many people in this society disliked.

Wittipol (the Spanish lady) said, "And you would have your wife be a lady of spirit, or a woman of fashion!"

"Yes, madam," Fitzdottrel replied. "I would have her be airy, somewhat light — not to plain dishonesty, I mean, but somewhat on this side."

A "light" woman was a promiscuous woman. Fitzdottrel wanted his wife to be flirtatious enough to fit in with this society, but he did not want her to cuckold him.

"I understand you, sir," Wittipol (the Spanish lady) said.

He then said, "He has reason, ladies."

Just that morning, Wittipol had spoken to Fitzdottrel's wife and attempted to persuade her to commit adultery with him.

He kicked at a rush lying on the floor and said, "I'll not give this rush for any lady who cannot be honest within a thread."

A rush is a stalk or a leaf from plants called, yes, rushes. Rush mats were often placed on the floor. Wittipol was saying that he would not give a rush, which is something worthless, for a woman who did not know what she could get away with — that is, for a woman who could flirt and flirt and perhaps do more than flirt yet keep her reputation.

He was also referencing the rush mat that lay between him and Mrs. Frances Fitzdottrel that morning.

Lady Tailbush said, "Yes, madam, and yet venture as far for the other, in her reputation —"

Wittipol (the Spanish lady) interrupted, "— as can be."

Sneaky women could keep their reputations, yet still do many, many things that respectable women ought not to do.

Wittipol (the Spanish lady) listed some of those things:

"Coach it to the resort town of Pimlico.

"Dance the scandalous dance called the saraband.

"Hear bawdy language and talk bawdy language.

"Laugh as loudly as an alarm clock.

"Squeak, spring, do anything —"

Squeaking could be done in bed.

The verb "spring" has some meanings that could refer to the act of sex or what can follow the act of sex: 1) moving energetically and changing position, 2) undergoing flushing of the skin, 3) causing water to rise (sweating), 4) being covered with water (semen), and 5) suffering the spreading of a rumor.

Or perhaps "squeak, spring" simply meant "sing, dance."

Lady Eitherside interrupted, "— in young company, madam."

Lady Tailbush added, "Or before gallants. If they are splendid, or lords, a woman is bound to do so."

"I say so, ladies," Fitzdottrel said. "It is civility to deny us nothing."

Pug, the devil from Hell, admired Fitzdottrel. He said to himself, "You talk of a university! Why, Hell is a grammar school compared to this!"

Lady Eitherside said, "But then she must not lose a look on stuffs, or cloth, madam."

"Stuffs" refers to materials for dresses, but readers may be forgiven for at first thinking that it refers to male parts that can be stuffed into lady parts.

"Nor no coarse fellow," Lady Tailbush said.

"She must be guided, madam, by the clothes he wears, and the company he is in," Wittipol (the Spanish lady) said. "Whom to salute, how far —"

Fitzdottrel interrupted, "I have told her — my wife —this. And I have told her that bawdy language, too, upon the point, is in itself as civil a discourse —"

Wittipol (the Spanish lady) interrupted, "— as any other affair of flesh, whatever."

To be a member of this particular crowd of people, you needed to speak bawdily and flirt outrageously, and perhaps do worse things. Fitzdottrel wanted his wife to be a member of this particular crowd of people.

Fitzdottrel continued, "But she will never be capable; she is not so much as coming, madam."

This can be interpreted in two ways:

1) "But she will never be capable of understanding that; she is not so much as coming around to understand that, madam."

2) "But she will never be capable of having such evil and effrontery; she is not so much as cumming, madam."

Fitzdottrel continued, "I don't know how she loses all her opportunities with hoping to be forced."

The word "forced" means "raped," but lesser kinds of force may include "seduced" or "persuaded."

Fitzdottrel was a jealous husband who was afraid that Wittipol would seduce his wife — and afraid that his wife wouldn't mind being seduced — and so he probably meant that he couldn't understand why his wife did not want to fit in with this particular crowd of people when she, herself, would not mind being seduced.

Fitzdottrel continued, "I've entertained a gentleman, a younger brother, here" — he pointed to Pug — "whom I would like to breed up as her *escudero*, in anticipation of some expectations that I have, and she'll not countenance him."

"What's his name?" Wittipol (the Spanish lady) asked.

"His name is Devil, and he's from Derbyshire," Fitzdottrel said.

Because of Pug's name, Lady Eitherside said, "Bless us from him!"

This meant: May God protect us from him.

"Devil?" Lady Tailbush said. "Call him De-vile, sweet madam."

"Call him whatever you please, ladies," Mrs. Frances Fitzdottrel said.

"De-vile's a prettier name!" Lady Tailbush said.

"And the name sounds, I think, as if it came in with William the Conqueror in the Norman Conquest," Lady Eitherside said.

Referring to Lady Tailbush and Lady Eitherside, a disgusted Manly said, "They are worse than smocks — prostitutes! What things they are! That nature should be at leisure ever to make people like them! My wooing is at an end. I will no longer woo Lady Tailbush."

Indignant, he exited.

Referring to Pug, Wittipol (the Spanish lady) asked, "What can he do?"

"Let's hear him," Lady Eitherside said.

"Can he manage?" Lady Tailbush asked.

One meaning of "manage" is "perform," perhaps meaning sexually. Another meaning of "manage" could be "manage an affair" — that is, be a good go-between for a lady and her lover.

"If it would please you to test him and ask him questions, ladies, do so," Fitzdottrel said.

He ordered, "Stand forth, Devil."

Pug said to himself, "Was all this but the preface to my torment?"

"Come, let Their Ladyships see your honors," Fitzdottrel said. "Let them see you bow."

Pug bowed.

"Oh, he makes a wicked leg," Lady Eitherside said.

A "wicked leg" is a badly performed bow.

"As wicked as ever I saw!" Lady Tailbush said.

"Fit for a Devil," Wittipol (the Spanish lady) said.

"Good madam, call him De-vile," Lady Tailbush requested.

They began a catechism — a question-and-answer test — of Pug.

Wittipol (the Spanish lady) asked Pug, "De-vile, what property is there most required in your opinion, now, while in service as a Spanish squire — an *escudero*?"

Pug hesitated.

Fitzdottrel asked him, "Why don't you speak?"

Pug then answered Wittipol (the Spanish lady), "Most required is a settled discreet pace, madam."

Wittipol (the Spanish lady) replied, "Most required, I think, is a barren head, sir, mountain-like, to be exposed to the cruelty of weathers —"

Many servants in the position of squire were required to be bareheaded. High mountains are bareheaded in the sense that trees will not grow above a certain elevation.

"Aye, for his valley is beneath the waste, madam, and to be fruitful there, it is sufficient," Fitzdottrel said.

According to Fitzdottrel, Pug's head was barren — a waste. Below Pug's waist was a valley, but it was a valley in back. What came out there would be fruitful if used to fertilize fruit trees.

Fitzdottrel then said to Pug, "Dullness upon you! Couldn't you hit this?"

"Hit this" meant "hit on the right answer."

Fitzdottrel hit Pug, who began, "Good sir —"

Wittipol (the Spanish lady) said, "If he had hit on the right answer, then he would have had no barren head! You torment him too much, indeed, sir."

Fitzdottrel said to Pug, "I must walk with a French stick, like an old verger, on account of you."

A French stick is a walking stick, and a verger is a public official who carried a rod as a symbol of his authority.

Fitzdottrel believed that because of Pug's ignorance, he had to carry a walking stick so he could use it to beat Pug.

Pug quietly prayed to Satan, "Oh, chief, call me back to Hell again, and free me!"

"Do you murmur now?" Fitzdottrel asked Pug.

"Not I, sir," Pug replied.

"What do you take to be, Master De-vile, the height of your employment in the true perfect service of the *escudero*?" Wittipol (the Spanish lady) asked Pug.

Again, Pug hesitated.

"When will you answer?" Fitzdottrel asked. "What do you answer?"

Pug answered Wittipol (the Spanish lady), "To be able, madam, first to inquire about and then to report the efficacy of any lady's medicine, using sweet phrases."

Some kinds of medicines are laxatives. Pug would be asking ladies whether their laxatives had worked.

Wittipol (the Spanish lady) said, "Yes, that's an act of elegance and importance. But what is above that? What is truer and more perfect service than that?"

"Oh, I wish that I had a goad to use on Pug!" Fitzdottrel said.

"To find a good cutter of ladies' corns," Pug said.

Insulted, Lady Tailbush said, "He can get out right now!"

"Most barbarous!" Lady Eitherside said.

"Why did you give this answer, now?" Fitzdottrel said to Pug. "On purpose to discredit me? You damned Devil!"

Pug said to himself, "Sure, if I am not yet a damned devil, I shall be. All my days in Hell were holy-days compared to this!"

"This is labor lost, madam," Lady Tailbush said.

"He's a dull fellow of no intellectual capacity," Lady Eitherside said.

"And of no discourse," Lady Tailbush added. "Oh, if my Ambler would have been here!"

"Yes, madam," Lady Eitherside said. "When you talk about Ambler, you talk about a man. Where is there such another?"

Wittipol (the Spanish lady) said, "Master De-vile, suppose that one of my ladies here had a fine bitch, and she wanted to employ you to go forth to entreat about a convenient match for her."

In other words, suppose that one of the ladies here had a female dog and was seeking a mate for it.

Wittipol (the Spanish lady) continued, "What would you observe that would help you to find a fine mate for it?"

"The color, and the size, madam," Pug said.

"And nothing else?" Wittipol (the Spanish lady) asked.

"The moon, you calf, the moon!" Fitzdottrel said.

He was calling Pug a mooncalf, aka a monster.

"Yes, the moon, and the astrological sign of the bitch," Pug said.

"Yes," Lady Tailbush said, "and recipes for aphrodisiacs."

"Then when the puppies came, what would you do?" Wittipol (the Spanish lady) asked.

"Get their nativities — horoscopes — cast," Pug answered.

"This is well," Wittipol (the Spanish lady) said. "What else?"

"Consult the almanac-man about which would be the smallest? And which would be the cleanliest?" Pug answered.

"And which the silentest?" Wittipol (the Spanish lady) asked.

Lady Tailbush said, "This is well, madam!"

Wittipol (the Spanish lady) asked Pug, "And what would you do while she were pregnant with puppies?"

Pug answered, "Walk her outside, and air her every morning."

"Very good!" Wittipol (the Spanish lady) said. "And be industrious to kill her fleas?"

"Yes," Pug said.

"He will make a pretty student," Wittipol (the Spanish lady) said.

Pug said to himself, "Who, coming from Hell, could look for such catechizing? The devil is an ass. I do acknowledge it."

Which devil? Possibly, Pug himself. He had acted foolishly in wishing to leave Hell in order to visit earth.

Fitzdottrel, impressed by Wittipol (the Spanish lady), said to himself, "The top of woman! All her sex in abstract! I love each syllable that falls from her!"

Referring to Pug, Lady Tailbush requested, "Good madam, give me permission to go aside with him and test him a little."

"Do, and I'll withdraw, madam, with this fair lady — and teach her the while," Wittipol (the Spanish lady) said.

Lady Tailbush said to Pug, "Come with me, sir."

Pug prayed quietly, "Dear chief, relieve me, or I perish!"

"Lady, we'll follow you two," Wittipol (the Spanish lady) said.

Lady Tailbush and Lady Eitherside exited with Pug.

Wittipol (the Spanish lady) asked Fitzdottrel, "You are not jealous of me being with your wife, sir?"

Because Fitzdottrel thought that Wittipol (the Spanish lady) was a woman, he replied, "Oh, madam! You shall see."

He said to his wife, "Stay, wife."

Mrs. Frances Fitzdottrel had disliked the company and she had disliked Pug's being teased and beaten, and she wanted to leave and go to her home. She had no desire to be taught to behave like Lady Tailbush and Lady Eitherside.

Fitzdottrel said to Wittipol (the Spanish lady), "Behold, I give her up here absolutely to you. She is your own. Do with her what you will."

He put his wife's arm in the arm of Wittipol (the Spanish lady).

Using a metaphor from metalworking, Fitzdottrel added, "Melt, cast, and form her as you shall think good. Set any stamp on her. I'll receive her from you as a new thing, by your own standard!"

He exited.

"Well, sir!" Wittipol (the Spanish lady) said.

Wittipol (the Spanish lady) and Mrs. Frances Fitzdottrel exited.

Merecraft and Fitzdottrel talked together.

"But what have you done in your dependence, since we last talked about it?" Merecraft asked.

The dependence was Fitzdottrel's quarrel with Wittipol.

"Oh, it goes on," Fitzdottrel said. "I met your cousin, the Master —"

"You did not acquaint him, sir, with what you are now doing?" Merecraft asked.

He had advised Fitzdottrel to put his financial affairs in order and decide on a beneficiary, without consulting Everill.

Fitzdottrel replied, "Indeed, I did acquaint him with the facts, sir.

"And upon better thought, not without reason! He being chief officer might have taken it ill, if I had not. He might have taken it as an act of contempt against his office, and that in time, sir, might have drawn on another dependence — he and I might have had a quarrel."

Merecraft had told Fitzdottrel that Everill was going to be Master of the Dependences, and so Fitzdottrel had thought it best to keep Everill informed about his dependence.

Fitzdottrel continued, "I did find him in good terms, and ready to do me any service."

"So he said to you!" Merecraft said. "But sir, you do not know him."

Fitzdottrel said, "Why, I presumed because this business of my wife's required me to act, I could not have done better than consult Everill; and he told me that he would go immediately to your counsel, a knight, here, in the lane —"

"Yes, Justice Eitherside," Merecraft said.

Fitzdottrel continued, "And get the deed of feoffment drawn, with a letter of attorney for livery and seisin."

A deed of feoffment is a deed of freehold. "Livery and seisin" is a legal term for the delivery of property.

With these documents, an unscrupulous person could gain possession of Fitzdottrel's entire estate. More than one con man wanted to gain possession of Fitzdottrel's entire estate.

"That I know is the course of action." Merecraft said. "But sir, you don't mean to make him feoffee, do you?"

In other words: Do you intend to give Everill control of your entire estate?

Fitzdottrel said, "Nay, that I'll pause on."

Pitfall, Lady Tailbush's female attendant, entered the room.

"What is it now, little Pitfall!" Merecraft asked.

"Your cousin Master Everill wants to come in — but he wants to know first whether Master Manly is here," Pitfall said.

"No, tell Everill that Manly is not here," Merecraft said. "Tell Everill that if Manly were here, I have made his peace."

Actually, Manly still greatly disliked Everill — and Merecraft.

Pitfall exited.

Merecraft said quietly to Fitzdottrel about Everill, "He's one, sir, who has no estate, and a man doesn't know how such a trust may tempt him."

"I understand what you are saying," Fitzdottrel said.

Everill might be — make that definitely would be — tempted to misuse Fitzdottrel's estate to benefit himself if he were to get control of it.

Everill and Plutarchus entered the room.

Everill said, "Sir, this same deed is done here."

The deed was the deed of feoffment — the deed of freehold.

"Pretty Plutarchus!" Merecraft said. "Have thou come with it? And has Sir Paul Eitherside viewed it?"

"His signature is on the draft," Plutarchus said.

Merecraft asked Fitzdottrel, "Will you step in, sir, and read it?"

"Yes," Fitzdottrel said.

"Please, let me have a word with you," Everill said to Fitzdottrel.

He took him aside and whispered, "Sir Paul Eitherside wanted me to tell you to be cautious about whom you will make feoffee, for this is the trust of your whole estate; and although my cousin here is a worthy gentleman, yet his valor — his ability to pay his debts — has at the gambling board been questioned, and we believe any man so impeached to be of doubtful honesty. I will not confirm the truth of this information, but I give it to you to make your profit of it. If you utter it, I can forswear it and deny that I ever told this to you."

Fitzdottrel replied, "I believe you, and I thank you, sir."

Everyone exited.

Wittipol and Mrs. Frances Fitzdottrel talked together.

Although Wittipol was still dressed as the Spanish lady, he had revealed his true identity to her.

He said, "Don't be afraid, sweet lady. You're entrusted to love, not violence here: I am no ravisher, just one whom you, by your fair trust again, may of a servant make a most true friend."

A ravisher is a rapist.

In this context, a servant is an admirer, and a friend is a lover.

"And such a one I need, but not in this way," Mrs. Frances Fitzdottrel said.

She meant that she needed a most true friend but not a most true lover.

Manly snuck into the room, unnoticed, and hid.

Mrs. Frances Fitzdottrel continued, "Sir, let me confess to you that the splendid manner of your attempting this morning to persuade me to commit adultery with you intrigued me, and I acknowledge that my ability to devise plans and my manners were both engaged to give it a response — but not the response that you wanted. I never considered committing adultery.

"My hope was then — although it was interrupted before it could be uttered — that you whom I found to be the master of such language, that you who had the brain and the spirit for such an enterprise, could not but, if those good things were demanded to be used in a morally right cause, employ them virtuously, and make that profit of your noble qualities that they would yield."

In other words, although Wittipol had been using his great gifts to attempt to do evil, she believed that he was capable of using his great gifts to do good.

She continued, "Sir, you have now the ground and cause to exercise them in — you can use your great gifts to do good.

"I am a woman who cannot speak more wretchedness of myself than you can read in my features and my life. I am matched — married — to a mass of folly — my husband — who every day hastens to his own ruin.

"The wealthy portion — my dowry — that I brought to him, he has spent, and, through my friends' neglect, no jointure has been made for me."

The jointure she meant was shared control of their estate, with the proviso that if she became a widow, she would have wealth enough to support herself.

She wanted to be able to restrain her husband's foolish losses of money. His wasteful spending and loss of money to astrologers and con men were threatening to impoverish them.

Mrs. Frances Fitzdottrel continued, "My fortunes standing in this precipice, it is counsel that I want, and honest aides. And in this way, I need you for a friend, never in any other meaning of the word — I don't need a lover. My husband's ill — his evil — must not make me, sir, worse."

Manly, who had been eavesdropping while hidden, now revealed himself to Mrs. Frances Fitzdottrel and his friend Wittipol.

"Oh, friend, don't forsake the splendid occasion virtue offers you to keep you innocent!" Manly said. "I have feared for both of you, and I have been watching you so I could prevent the ill I feared. But since the weaker side — the woman — has so assured me, let not the stronger fall by his own vice, or be the less a friend because virtue needs him."

Manly was a good man, and he had been worried because his friend Wittipol wanted to commit adultery, which meant corrupting another man's wife. Now Wittipol had a chance to do good for the woman he had been trying to persuade to do evil, and Manly wanted Wittipol to take advantage of the opportunity to do good.

Wittipol, although he had been tempted to do evil, was basically a good man. He said, "Virtue shall never ask for my help twice. Most friend, most man, your counsels are commands."

Wittipol had been looking out for Manly by showing him that the woman he was wooing — Lady Tailbush — was not a morally good woman. Manly was looking out for Wittipol by advising him to act virtuously and help Mrs. Frances Fitzdottrel.

Both men appreciated the true friendship of the other.

Wittipol said to Mrs. Frances Fitzdottrel, "Lady, I can love the goodness in you more than I loved your beauty, and I here entitle your virtue to the power upon a life you shall engage in any fruitful service, even if it means forfeiting my life."

He would help her, even if it meant losing his life.

Merecraft entered the room and said, "Madam."

Mrs. Frances Fitzdottrel curtsied and then exited.

Merecraft took aside Wittipol, who was still dressed as the Spanish lady, and whispered to him, "Listen, sir. We have another leg strained — another plot activated — for this Dottrel. He has a quarrel to carry, and he has caused a deed of feoffment of his whole estate to be drawn yonder. He has the deed of feoffment within; and he intends to make feoffee only you: the Spanish lady. He's fallen so desperately in love with you, and talks almost like a madman — you have never heard a frantic lunatic so in love with his own fancy! Now, as you know, the deed of feoffment will have no validity if it is in the Spanish lady's name; therefore, I want you to advise Fitzdottrel to put the deed of feoffment in my name and give me control of his estate — here he comes — you shall have a share of his estate, sir."

Fitzdottrel, Everill, and Plutarchus entered the room. Plutarchus was holding the deed of feoffment. No one had yet been named the feoffee: A blank space had been left in the document for the name or names to be entered later.

One might think that Fitzdottrel would name his wife as feoffee and let her have control of their estate rather than signing legal control of the estate over to a guardian, but Fitzdottrel did not consider this. Apparently, he did not love or respect — or trust — his wife enough for him to do this.

Fitzdottrel said to Wittipol (the Spanish lady), "Madam, I have a request to make to you, and before I make the request I say this to you: You must not deny me; I will be granted what I request."

In other words: I won't take no for an answer.

"Sir, I must know what you are asking me to do, though," Wittipol (the Spanish lady) said.

"No, lady, you must not know it," Fitzdottrel said, "Yet you must know it, too, for the trust of it, and the fame indeed, which otherwise would be lost to me. I want to use your name in a deed of feoffment — I want to make my whole estate over to you: My whole estate is a trifle, a thing of nothing, some eighteen hundred pounds a year in income."

"Alas!" Wittipol (the Spanish lady) said. "I don't understand those things, sir. I am a woman, and I am most loathe to embark myself —"

"You will not slight me, madam?" Fitzdottrel asked.

"Nor will you quarrel with me?" Wittipol (the Spanish lady) asked.

"No, sweet madam, I have already a dependence — a quarrel — which is the reason I am doing this. Let me put you in the deed of feoffment, dear madam. As a result of my quarrel, I may be fairly killed."

The quarrel could result in a duel and yes, Fitzdottrel might die in the duel, and so he needed to settle his estate and find a guardian for it before fighting the duel.

"You have your friends, sir, around you here," Wittipol (the Spanish lady) said. "You may choose one of them as the feoffee."

Hoping to be named the feoffee, Everill said to Fitzdottrel, "She tells you right, sir."

Fitzdottrel replied, "By God's death, so what if she does — what do I care for that? Tell her that I want her to tell me wrong."

Wittipol (the Spanish lady) said, "Why, sir, if you want a recommendation for the trust, you may let me have the honor to name you whom I recommend."

"It is you who do me the honor, madam," Fitzdottrel said. "Who is it whom you recommend?"

"This gentleman," Wittipol (the Spanish lady) said, pointing to Manly.

"Oh, no, sweet madam," Fitzdottrel said. "He's a friend to the man with whom I have the dependence — the quarrel."

Wittipol (the Spanish lady) asked, "Who might he be?"

"He is named Wittipol," Fitzdottrel replied, "Do you know him?"

"Alas, sir, he is just a toy, a trifle — you think that this gentleman is a friend to him?" Wittipol (the Spanish lady) said. "He is no more a friend to Wittipol than I am, sir!"

"But will Your Ladyship vouch for that, madam?" Fitzdottrel asked.

"Yes, and whatever else for him you will engage me," Wittipol (the Spanish lady) said.

"What is his name?" Fitzdottrel asked.

"His name is Eustace Manly," Wittipol (the Spanish lady) said.

"From where does he write himself?" Fitzdottrel asked.

"He is Eustace Manly of Middlesex, Esquire," Wittipol (the Spanish lady) said.

"Say no more, madam," Fitzdottrel said.

He then said to Plutarchus, "Clerk, come here. Write 'Eustace Manly, squire of Middlesex' as the feoffee on the deed of feoffment."

Plutarchus wrote the name on the document and then gave it to Manly.

Merecraft whispered to Wittipol, "What have you done, sir?"

Wittipol whispered back, "I have named a gentleman for whom I'll be answerable to you, sir. Had I named you, it might have raised suspicions. This way, all is safe."

Fitzdottrel said, "Come, gentlemen, write your signatures as witnesses."

"What is this?" Manly asked. He disliked both Merecraft and Everill, who would sign the deed of feoffment as witnesses.

Everill said to Fitzdottrel, "You have made election of a most worthy gentleman."

He was pretending to approve of Manly's being selected as the feoffee on the deed of feoffment.

"I wish that a worthy man had said that!" Manly said to Everill. "Considering the man from whom it comes, it is rather a shame to me than a praise."

"Sir, I will give you any satisfaction," Everill said.

The satisfaction could be a duel, but Manly preferred silence.

"Be silent then," Manly said. "Falsehood does not commend the truth."

Plutarchus said to Fitzdottrel, "Do you deliver this, sir, as your deed to the use of Master Manly? Do you want him to be the feoffee on the deed of feoffment?"

"Yes," Fitzdottrel said.

He then said to Manly, "And sir, when did you see young Wittipol? I am ready for process now; sir, this is publication of my quarrel. He shall hear from me; he would necessarily be courting my wife, sir."

Manly said, "Yes, his cloak, which you are wearing, witnesses that what you say is true."

This remark made Fitzdottrel suspicious of Manly, and he said to him, "Nay, good sir."

Fitzdottrel then said to Wittipol (the Spanish lady), "Madam, you did assert —"

Wittipol (the Spanish lady) interrupted, "What?"

Fitzdottrel finished, "— that he was not Wittipol's friend."

"I have heard, sir, no confession of it," Wittipol (the Spanish lady) replied.

He had not heard Manley confess that he was not Wittipol's friend.

Fitzdottrel said to himself, "Oh, she doesn't know the facts of the matter!"

He then said to Wittipol (the Spanish lady), "Now I remember, madam! This young Wittipol would have debauched my wife and made me a cuckold through a window; he did pursue her to her home to my own window; but I think I swooped on him, and violently moved her away from out of his claws. I have sworn to have him by the ears; I fear the toy will not do right by me."

He was saying that he wanted to meet Wittipol in a duel, but he was afraid that Wittipol would not fight him.

"He won't do right by you?" Wittipol (the Spanish lady) replied. "That would be a pity! What right do you ask, sir? Here is the man who will do right by you."

Wittipol revealed his real identity; he no longer pretended to be the Spanish lady.

"Ha?" Fitzdottrel said. "Wittipol?"

"Aye, sir," Wittipol said. "I am a lady no more now, nor am I a Spaniard."

"No, indeed," Manly said. "This is Wittipol."

"Am I the thing I feared you would make me?" Fitzdottrel asked.

"A cuckold?" Wittipol said. "No, sir, but you were recently in possibility, I'll tell you so much."

He meant that he had recently had a possible opportunity to make Fitzdottrel a cuckold.

Good man that he was, Manly clarified, "But your wife's too virtuous to make you a cuckold."

"We'll see her, sir, safely to her home, and leave you here to be made the Duke of Shoreditch with a project," Wittipol said.

"Duke of Shoreditch" was a joke title; no real such Duke existed.

"Thieves! Ravishers!" Fitzdottrel said.

"Cry just one more note, sir, and I'll mar the tune of your pipe," Wittipol said.

Fitzdottrel said, "Give me my deed of feoffment, then."

Wittipol told him, "No. That shall be kept for the good of your wife, who will know better than you how to use it."

Manly would not use the deed of feoffment to benefit himself; it would be used to benefit Mrs. Frances Fitzdottrel. Doing so would also benefit Fitzdottrel, although he did not believe that.

Fitzdottrel thought about how he believed his wife would better know how to use it: "To feast you with my land?"

"Sir, be quiet, or I shall gag you before I go," Wittipol said. "Consult your Master of Dependences about how to make this a second quarrel. You have time, sir."

Wittipol shoved Fitzdottrel out of the way, and he and Manly exited.

"Oh!" Fitzdottrel said. "What will the ghost of my wise grandfather, my learned father, and my worshipful mother think about me now, they who left me in this world in state to be their heir? They will think that I have become a cuckold, and an ass, and my wife's ward, and they will think that I am likely to lose my land and have my throat cut, all by her scheming!"

"Sir, we are all abused," Merecraft said.

"And continue to be so!" Fitzdottrel said. "Who hinders you? Please, let me alone. I would 'enjoy' myself and be the Duke of Drowned-land you have made me."

"Sir, we must play an after-game concerning this," Merecraft said.

An after-game was a second game played to make up the losses suffered in the first game.

"But I am in no condition to be a gambler," Fitzdottrel said. Because of the deed of feoffment, he had no money, no possessions, and no land.

He continued, "I tell you once again —"

Merecraft interrupted, "You must be ruled by me and take some counsel."

He would advise Fitzdottrel about how to recover his estate.

Fitzdottrel replied, "Sir, I hate counsel, as I hate my wife, my wicked wife!"

"But we may think of a way for you to recover all your estate, if you will act," Merecraft said.

"I will not think, nor act, nor yet recover," Fitzdottrel said. "Do not talk to me! I'll run out of my wits rather than listen to you. I will be what I am, Fabian Fitzdottrel, although all the world say nay to it."

He exited.

Merecraft said to Everill, "Let's follow him."

CHAPTER 5
— 5.1 —

Outside Lady Tailbush's house, Ambler and Pitfall talked together. Ambler, Lady Tailbush's manservant, had been missing all day, and he was worried about losing his job.

"But has my lady missed me?" Ambler asked.

"Beyond telling!" Pitfall said. "Here has been that infinity of strangers! And then she would have had you to have used you as a good model compared with one inside whom they are now teaching, and who is ambitious to be of your rank."

"Good fellow-servant Pitfall, tell Master Merecraft that I entreat a word with him."

Pitfall exited.

Alone, Ambler said to himself, "This most unlucky accident will go near to be the loss of my job, I fear!"

Merecraft entered the scene.

"A word with me?" Merecraft said. "What do you want to say to me, Master Ambler?"

"Sir, I would beseech Your Worship to protect me from my Lady Tailbush's displeasure at my absence," Ambler said.

"Oh, is that all?" Merecraft said. "I promise you that I will."

"I want to tell you, sir, just how it happened," Ambler said.

"Be brief, good Master Ambler, put yourself to your rack and exert yourself to be brief, for I have work of more importance to attend to."

"Sir, you'll laugh at me," Ambler said. "But — it is the truth — a true friend of mine, finding by conversation with me that I lived too chastely for my health, and indeed too honest for my place, sir, advised me that if I loved myself — as I do, I must confess —"

"Spare me your parenthetical remarks," Merecraft said. "Get to the point."

"That I should give my body a little evacuation —"

Occasionally, testicles ought to be emptied of semen.

"Well, and you went to a whore?" Merecraft asked.

"No, sir," Ambler said. "I dared not, for fear gossip might arrive at somebody's ear. I would not entrust myself to a common whorehouse."

He then spoke this rapidly:

"But I got the gentlewoman to go with me and carry her bedding to a conduit-head close by the place toward Tyburn that they call my Lord Mayor's Banqueting House.

"Now, sir, this morning there was a public execution at Tyburn, and I never dreamt of it until I heard the noise of the people and the horses, and neither I nor the poor gentlewoman dared to stir until all was done and past, so that in the interim we fell asleep again."

The conduit brought drinking water to London. The conduit-head had places where a couple could hide and have sex.

Out of breath, he stopped speaking.

"Nay, if you fall from your gallop, I am gone, sir," Merecraft said.

Ambler rapidly continued, "But when I waked to put on my clothes — a suit I had had made for the occasion — it was gone, and so was all my money, with my purse, my seals, my notebooks, my studies, and a fine new device I had to carry my pen and ink, my civet perfume, and my toothpicks, all in one case. But that which grieved me most was the thefts of the gentlewoman's shoes, with a pair of roses and garters I had given her for the business."

Ambler continued, "So that made us stay until it was dark, for I was obliged to lend her my shoes, and walk in a rug by her, barefoot to Saint Giles' church."

"A kind of Irish penance!" Merecraft said.

Some impoverished Irish wore clothing made out of rug cloth.

Merecraft then asked, "Is this all, sir?"

"I want you to satisfy Lady Tailbush that I deserve to keep my job," Ambler replied.

"I promise you that I will, sir," Merecraft said.

"I have told you my true disaster," Ambler said.

"I cannot stay with you, sir, to console you, but I rejoice in your return," Merecraft said.

He went inside.

"He is an honest gentleman!" Ambler said. "But he's never at leisure to relax and be himself because he has such tides of business."

He went inside.

Alone, Pug said to himself, "Oh, call me home again, dear chief, and put me to work yoking foxes, milking he-goats, pounding water in a mortar, emptying the sea dry with a nutshell, gathering all the leaves that have fallen this autumn, drawing farts out of dead bodies, making ropes out of sand, catching the winds together in a net, mustering ants, and numbering atoms — all that Hell and you thought exquisite torments, rather than keep me here for the length of time it takes to think a thought! I would sooner keep fleas within a circle and keep track for a thousand years which of them out-leaped the other and by how far, than endure a minute more of such torment as I have suffered within this house. There is no Hell compared to a lady of fashion — all your tortures in Hell are enjoyable pastimes compared to spending time with a lady of fashion! It would be refreshing for me to be in hellfire again and away from here!"

Ambler entered the scene, looked at him, and said to himself, "This man is wearing my suit, and those are the gentlewoman's shoes and roses!"

Apparently, Pug had small feet, and so he had stolen the gentlewoman's shoes rather than Ambler's shoes. Small feet may be a cause of the myth saying the devils have cloven hooves rather than feet.

"They have such impertinent vexations that a general council of devils could not hit on," Pug continued.

He noticed Ambler and said to himself, "Ha! This is the man I took asleep with his wench and borrowed his clothes. What might I do to frustrate him?"

"Do you hear me, sir?" Ambler asked.

Pug said to himself, "Answer him, but not to the purpose."

"What is your name, I ask you, sir?" Ambler asked.

"Is it so late, sir?" Pug said, deliberately not answering the question.

"I ask you not for the time, but for your name, sir," Ambler said.

"I thank you, sir," Pug said. "Yes, it does hold, sir, certainly."

"Hold, sir?" Ambler said. "What holds? I must both hold and talk to you about these clothes you are wearing."

"A very pretty lace!" Pug said. "But the tailor cheated me."

"No, I am cheated by you!" Ambler said. "Robbed!"

"Why, when you please, sir, I am ready for the game of threepenny gleek," Pug said. "I am your man for that."

"A pox on your gleek and threepence!" Ambler said. "Give me an answer."

"Sir, my master is the best at it," Pug said.

"Your master!" Ambler said. "Who is your master?"

"Let it be Friday night," Pug said.

"What should be then?" Ambler asked.

"Your best song's 'Tom o' Bedlam,'" Pug said.

A Tom o' Bedlam was a lunatic who had been released from Bethlem Royal Hospital and licensed so he could beg.

"I think you are he," Ambler said to Pug.

He then asked himself, "Does he mock me on purpose, I wonder? Or am I not speaking to him what I mean?"

He then said to Pug, "Good sir, what is your name?"

"Only a couple of cocks, sir," Pug said. "If we can get a widgeon, it is in season."

Widgeons were a species of bird that was in season in England during autumn.

Ambler said to himself, "He hopes to make one of these Sciptics of me — I think I got their name right — and he does not flee from me. I wonder at that! It is a strange confidence!"

By "Sciptics" he meant Skeptics — philosophers who did not think that knowledge was objective.

Ambler continued saying to himself, "I'll try another way to draw a real answer from him."

Ambler exited.

Merecraft, Fitzdottrel, and Everill entered the scene. Pug withdrew to a space where he could hear but was unlikely to be seen. He listened to everything the newcomers said.

Merecraft was trying to convince Fitzdottrel to say that his wife was a witch who had caused him to become possessed by a demon. If his wife was brought to trial and convicted as a witch, she would be unable to control her husband's property.

Who would then control Fitzdottrel's property? If Fitzdottrel were thought to be bewitched, he would not be able to. Both Merecraft and Everill, of course, were eager to control Fitzdottrel's property. At this time, Fitzdottrel still did not know that Merecraft and Everill were con men.

"It is the easiest thing, sir, to be done," Merecraft said to Fitzdottrel. "It is as simple as farting silently."

This is not always easy to do. So the author of the book you are reading has heard.

Merecraft continued, "Roll your eyes, and foam at the mouth. A little Castile soap will do for foam — rub it on your lips. And then get a nutshell with inflammable fibers and tinder in it so you can spit fire."

Presumably, the "possessed" person would be able to secretly get the finely ground fibers and tinder from the nutshell to his lips, and then spray them into a fireplace or over the flame of a candle, creating a fireball and conveying the impression to bystanders that he had spit fire.

Merecraft continued, "Did you never read, sir, about little Darrel's tricks, the boy of Burton, the seven in Lancashire, and Sommers at Nottingham? All these people's histories teach these tricks. And we'll say, sir, that your wife has bewitched you —"

These people had faked or convinced others to fake being bewitched.

John Darrel had performed exorcisms on people and had caused a man to be executed. In 1599 he was accused of being an imposter and was imprisoned.

The boy of Burton was Thomas Darling, who had pretended to be bewitched and had claimed that a mouse had come out of his mouth.

Seven children in Lancashire were supposedly bewitched when a man named Edward (or perhaps Edmund) Hartley kissed them and breathed evil spirits in them.

William Sommers of Nottingham was also supposed to have been bewitched. John Darrel exorcized him.

Everill said, "And we'll say that your wife conspired with those two, as sorcerers."

"Those two" were Wittipol and Manly.

Merecraft said, "And we'll say that they gave you potions, by which means you were not *compos mentis* — of sound mind — when you made your feoffment. There's no recovery of your estate unless you do this. This, sir, will sting; it will be fatal."

The punishment for being found guilty of witchcraft was death.

Everill added, "And it will move in a court of equity."

Such a court could overrule both common law and statute law — as well as common sense.

"For it is more than manifest that this was a plot of your wife's to get your land," Merecraft said.

"I think that is true," Fitzdottrel said.

"Sir, so it appears," Everill said.

Merecraft said, "Indeed, and my cousin has known these gallants in these shapes —"

Everill finished the sentence: "— to have done strange things, sir. One as the lady, the other as the squire."

They were referring to Wittipol and Manly. They were saying that Wittipol had dressed as a lady, and Manly had been her squire.

The squire could be a personal servant or a lover.

"How a man's honesty may be fooled!" Merecraft said. "I thought that he was a real lady."

"So did I — renounce me and cast me aside if I did not," Fitzdottrel said.

"But this way, sir, you'll be revenged in full," Merecraft said.

"Upon them all," Everill added.

"Yes, indeed," Merecraft said, "and since your wife has run the way of woman thus, even give her —"

Fitzdottrel interrupted, "— she is lost, I swear by this hand of mine, to me. She is dead to all the joys of her dear Dottrel! I shall never pity her who could pity herself. I cannot pity a woman who puts her own interests first because she pities herself."

"That is princely resolved, sir," Merecraft said, "and like yourself still, *in potentia.*"

Fitzdottrel was still not a duke; he was only potentially a duke. According to Merecraft, Fitzdottrel was acting like the duke he would soon be.

Pug, standing hidden, had overheard the plot.

Gilthead, Plutarchus (Gilthead's son), the constable Sledge, and some sergeants of the law arrived on the scene.

Merecraft asked, "Gilthead, what is the news?"

Fitzdottrel, who was in need of money, asked for the hundred pieces Gilthead was supposed to have given him earlier: "Oh, sir, my hundred pieces. Let me have them yet."

"Yes, sir," Gilthead replied.

He then said, "Officers of the law, arrest him."

"Me?" Fitzdottrel asked.

"I arrest you," a sergeant said.

"Keep the peace, I order you, gentlemen," the constable Sledge said.

"Arrest me?" Fitzdottrel said. "Why?"

"For better security, sir," Gilthead said. "My son Plutarchus assures me you're not worth a groat. Your net worth is not even a small coin of little value."

"Pardon me, father," Plutarchus said. "I said His Worship had no foot of land left, and that I'll justify, for I wrote the deed of feoffment."

Gilthead had placed Plutarchus, his son, with Sir Paul Eitherside so that he could learn law.

"Do you have these tricks in the city?" Fitzdottrel asked. He was a squire of Norfolk and so was not a citizen of London.

"Yes, and more," Gilthead said.

Pointing at Merecraft, he then said to the officers of the law, "Arrest this gallant, too, here, at my suit."

"Aye, and at mine," Sledge said. "He owes me for his lodging rent two years and a quarter."

Apparently, being a con man doesn't pay well, or if it does, it does so only occasionally.

Merecraft said, "Why, Master Gilthead, and landlord ... thou are not mad, though thou are constable. Thou are not puffed up with the pride of the place. Isn't that right? Do you hear me, sirs? Have I deserved this from you two for all my pains at court to get you each a patent — a monopoly?"

Gilthead asked, "A patent for what?"

"A patent concerning my project of the forks," Merecraft replied.

Forks were not yet widely in use in London and England.

"Forks?" Sledge asked. "What are forks?"

Instead of saying what forks were, Merecraft mentioned some of the advantages of forks: Less food would be spilled, and so less linen and less washing would be needed.

Merecraft said, "The laudable use of forks, brought into custom here, as they are in Italy, to the sparing of napkins. Sledge, this project would have made your bellows go at the forge, as it would have made Gilthead's go at the furnace. I had procured it, had the signet for it, dealt with the linen-drapers in private because I feared they were the likeliest to ever stir against it and to cross it, for it will be a mighty saver of linen through the kingdom — as that is one of my reasons for promoting the project, and to spare washing — now, on you two I had laid all the profits. Gilthead would have the making of all those forks made of gold and silver for the better personages, and you would have the making of those forks made of steel for the common sort. And both of you would have monopolies by patent. I would have brought you your seals in. But now you have prevented me from doing that, and I 'thank' you."

Sledge was persuaded by Merecraft's words that Merecraft was trying to help Sledge — and Gilthead — make money.

"Sir, I will provide bail for you at my own risk," Sledge said.

Merecraft said to Gilthead, "Choose what you will do."

Plutarchus said to Gilthead, "You do the same thing as Sledge, too, good father."

"I like the fashion of the project well," Gilthead said. "The forks! It may be a lucky project! And it is not complicated and intricate, as one would say, but fit for plain heads as ours to deal in."

He then said, "Listen to me, officers — we discharge you."

The officers of the law exited. Sledge stayed.

Merecraft said, "Why, this shows a little good nature in you, I confess, but do not tempt your friends thus."

He then said to Plutarchus, "Little Gilthead, advise your sire, great Gilthead, to avoid such courses of action as this action he almost did, and such courses of action as troubling a great man in reversion — a great man who is about to reclaim all his wealth — over a matter of fifty pounds on a false alarm.

Away with such courses of action! They do not show him in a good light. Let him get the hundred pieces and bring them here. You'll hear more else."

Plutarchus said, "Father!"

Gilthead and Plutarchus exited.

Ambler entered the scene. Seeing Pug, he dragged him out of hiding, and then he said, "Oh, Master Sledge, are you here? I have been to seek you. You are the constable, they say. Here's one whom I charge with felony, on account of the suit he is wearing, sir."

"Who?" Merecraft said. "Master Fitzdottrel's manservant? Beware what you are doing, Master Ambler."

"Sir, these clothes that he is wearing, I'll swear, are mine," Ambler said, "and he has on the shoes of the gentlewoman I told you of, and I will have him before a justice of the law."

"My master, sir, will pass his word for me," Pug said. "He will vouch for me."

"Oh, can you speak to the purpose now?" Ambler said sarcastically. "*Now* you can talk sense."

Fitzdottrel did not vouch for Pug; instead, he said to him, "Not I. If you are such a thief, sir, I will leave you to your godfathers-in-law. Let twelve men work."

The twelve godfathers-in-law were jurists. Fitzdottrel was willing for Pug to be brought to trial. If he were found guilty, he would be sentenced to death.

"Listen to me, sir," Pug said. "Please, let's talk in private."

They moved away from the others and talked quietly.

"Well, what do you say?" Fitzdottrel said. "Be brief, for I have no time to lose."

Pug replied, "The truth is, sir, I am truly a devil, and I had permission to take this body I am in to serve you, which belonged to a cutpurse who was hanged this morning. And it is likewise true that I stole this suit in order to clothe myself. But, sir, don't let me go to prison for it. I have hitherto lost time and done nothing; I have shown, indeed, no part of my devil's nature. Now I will so help your malice against these parties. Now I will so advance the business that you have at hand of witchcraft and your possession, as if I myself were in you. Now I will teach you such tricks as how to make your belly swell and how to make your eyes turn, and how to foam, to stare, to gnash your teeth together, and to beat yourself, to laugh loud, and to feign six voices —"

"Get out, you rogue!" Fitzdottrel said. "You most infernal counterfeit wretch! Get out! Do you think to gull me with your Aesop's fables?"

He did not believe that Pug was a real devil.

He said to the constable Sledge, "Here, take him into your custody; I want no part of him."

Pug began, "Sir —"

"Go away!" Fitzdottrel said. "I disclaim you. I will not listen to you."

Sledge led Pug away to take him to prison.

"What did he say to you, sir?" Merecraft asked.

"Like a lying rascal, he told me he was the devil," Fitzdottrel said.

"What!" Merecraft said. "A good jest!"

"And he said that he would teach me very fine devils' tricks for our new resolution," Fitzdottrel said.

"Oh, pox on him!" Everill said. "It was excellently wisely done, sir, not to trust him."

"Why, even if he were the devil, we shall not need him, if you'll be advised," Merecraft said.

Merecraft and Everill would teach Fitzdottrel very fine devils' tricks for their new resolution.

Merecraft then laid out the plot:

"Fitzdottrel, go throw yourself on a bed, sir, and feign that you are ill. We'll not be seen with you until after you have a fit, and that is confirmed within.

"Everill, stay with the two ladies — Lady Tailbush and Lady Eitherside — and persuade them to assist us.

"I'll go to Justice Eitherside and tell him all about the 'bewitchment.' I mean that I will tell him that Fitzdottrel is bewitched.

"Trains shall seek out Engine, and the two of them will fill the town with the news of Fitzdottrel's 'bewitchment.'"

Using a nautical metaphor, Merecraft said, "Every cable is to be paid out. We must employ all our emissaries to spread the news now."

He meant that they must use every means to spread the news of the "bewitchment."

Merecraft then said to Fitzdottrel, "Sir, I will send you bladders and bellows."

The bellows would blow up the bladders, which Fitzdottrel would use to make it seem as if his belly were distended by a demon or demons within him.

"Sir, be confident," Merecraft added. "This is no hard thing to outdo the devil in. A thirteen-year-old boy made him an ass just the other day."

A boy named John Smith claimed to have been bewitched; this resulted in the executions of nine women in July 1616. King James I then exposed the boy as a faker.

"Making the devil an ass" means "doing more evil than the devil." Today, we might call such a person "the devil's asshole."

Fitzdottrel said, "Well, I'll begin to practice, and escape the imputation of being made a cuckold by my own act."

"You're right," Merecraft said. "You will."

Fitzdottrel exited.

Now that Everill and Merecraft were alone, they could talk openly.

"Come," Everill said, "admit that you have put yourself and your friends into a complete mess here, by dealing with new agents in new plots. Your complications have muddled everything up."

"Speak no more about that, sweet cousin," Merecraft said. He was embarrassed.

"What had you to do with this Wittipol and his pretending to be a lady?" Everill asked.

"Don't ask about that," Merecraft said. "It is over and done."

"You had some strain above E-la?" Everill asked.

"E-la" is a high note in music.

Merecraft admitted, "I had indeed."

"And now you crack because of it," Everill said.

To crack on a note means to attempt — but fail — to sing it. Merecraft had attempted to get all rather than part of Fitzdottrel's wealth, and now he was in danger of getting none of it unless this new plot worked.

"Don't upbraid me," Merecraft said. "Don't criticize me."

"Come, you must be criticized about it," Everill said. "You are so greedy always to grab more than you are able to get that you lose everything."

"That is right," Merecraft admitted. "What more do you want me to do than to admit that I am guilty? Now, give me your aid."

They exited.

Shackles, the jail keeper of Newgate Prison, brought Pug into a cell.

He said, "Here you are lodged, sir; you must send your garnish, if you'll be private."

The garnish was a bribe to the jail keeper for private accommodations.

Pug gave him some money and said, "There it is, sir. Leave me."

Shackles exited.

"To Newgate brought?" Pug said. "How the name of 'devil' is discredited in me! What a lost fiend shall I be on my return to Hell! My chief will roar in triumph, now that I have been on earth for a day and have done no notable deed except bring back here the body that was hanged this morning.

"Well! I wish that it were midnight so that I knew my fate."

At midnight, Pug was supposed to return to Hell and make his report to Satan, who would sentence him for accomplishing no notable evil while he was in the Land of the Living.

Pug continued, "I think that Time is drunk and sleeps. He is so still, and he doesn't move! I glory now in my torment. Neither can I expect it; I have it with my fact."

He was already being tormented even before returning to Hell. He was tormented by his lack of success among the living, and he was tormented by the fact that he had ended up in Newgate Prison although he was a devil. He also was tormented by the knowledge that Satan would punish him when he returned to Hell. What's worse, Time was moving so slowly that it dragged out his torment.

Iniquity the Vice entered the scene and said to Pug, "Child of Hell, be merry! Put a look on as round, boy, and as red as a cherry. Cast care behind thee and dance in thy fetters; They are ornaments, baby, that have graced thy betters.

"Look at me, and listen," Iniquity the Vice said. "Our chief salutes thee, and, lest the cold iron of your fetters should chance to confute thee, he has sent thee grant-parole by me to stay a month longer here on earth, so you can learn to welcome cold and hunger, child —"

"What?" Pug said. "Shall I stay here a month longer?"

"Yes, boy, until the legal Session, so that thou may be found guilty and have a triumphal egression," Iniquity the Vice said.

"A triumphal egression in a cart, to be hanged!" Pug said.

Theft was a capital crime, and those found guilty were taken in a cart to the place of execution, where they were hanged.

Iniquity the Vice said, "No, child, in a car — the chariot of triumph, which most of them are."

"Car" and "chariot" were fancy words for "cart."

Iniquity the Vice continued, "And in the meantime, you will be greasy and boozy and drunken, and nasty and filthy, and ragged and louse-y, with 'damn me,' 'renounce me,' and all the fine phrases that bring to Tyburn the plentiful gazes."

Thieves were taken in a cart from Newgate Prison to Tyburn to be hung. Often, many people lined the route to see the condemned prisoner.

"He is a devil!" Pug said. "And he may well be our chief devil! The great superior devil! On account of his malice, he may well be Arch-devil! I acknowledge him. He knew what I would suffer when he tied me up thus in a rogue's body, and he has — I thank him — his tyrannous pleasure on me, to confine me to the unlucky carcass of a cutpurse, wherein I could do nothing."

Satan entered the scene and upbraided Pug with his day's work:

"Impudent fiend, stop thy lewd mouth.

"Don't thou shame and tremble to lay thine own dull damned defects upon an innocent carcass there? Why, thou miserable slave, the spirit that possessed that flesh before you took it over put more true life in a finger and a thumb than thou have in the whole mass! Yet thou rebel and complain?

"What one attempt have thou made that is wicked enough, this day, that might be called worthy of thine own name, much less worthy the name of Satan, who sent thee?

"First, thou did help thyself get a beating from Fitzdottrel promptly, and with it thou also endangered thy tongue. You were afraid that you would have your tongue cut out. You are a devil, and yet you could not keep a body unbeaten for even one day! So much for that being for our credit.

"And to get revenge for it, you stopped, for anything thou know, a deed of darkness, which was an act of that egregious folly as no one sympathetic toward the devil could have thought of."

Pug had informed Fitzdottrel about the meeting at the windows of his wife and Wittipol. By doing that, he had possibly stopped an act of adultery.

Satan continued, "So much for your acting! But now for your suffering! Why, a man wearing a false beard and a reversible cloak cheated thee. Indeed, would your predecessor the cutpurse, do you think, have been taken advantage of like that? Damn thee! Thou have done much harm: Thou have let men know their strength and that they're able to out-do a devil that has been put in a body — this will forever be a scar upon our name!

"Whom have thou dealt with, woman or man, this day, but they have outdone thee in some way, and most have proved to be the better fiends?

"Yet you would be employed? Yes, Hell shall make you the spiritual leader of the cheaters with false dice!

"Or Hell shall make you the bawd-ledger — the resident ambassador for the pimps and whores — for this side of the town!

"No doubt you'll render a splendid account of things. Bane of your itch, and scratching for employment! I'll have brimstone — sulphur — to relieve it, to be sure, and I'll have fire to singe your fingernails off."

Devils prefer to keep their fingernails long.

Satan continued, "Except that I would not have such a damned dishonor stick on our state — the dishonor that a devil were hanged and could not save a body that he took from Tyburn, but that body must go there again — you would ride the cart to the gallows."

Satan then said to The Vice named Iniquity, "But up, away with him —"

Iniquity the Vice put Pug upon his back so he could carry him away, saying to him, "Mount, darling of darkness. My shoulders are broad; he that carries the fiend is sure of his load. The Devil was accustomed to carry away the Evil, but now the Evil carries away the Devil."

In the morality plays of the Middle Ages, the Devil carried away on his back the Vice or Evil.

They exited.

— 5.7 —

A great noise was heard in Newgate Prison. Frightened, Shackles the jail keeper and some other jail keepers came into Pug's jail cell. The body that Pug had occupied was lying on the floor.

"Oh, me!" Shackles said.

"What's this?" the first jail keeper asked.

"A piece of Justice Hall has broken down," the second jail keeper said.

"Phew!" the third jail keeper said. "What a steam of brimstone is here!"

"The prisoner who came in just now is dead!" the fourth jail keeper said.

"Ha?" Shackles said. "Where?"

"Look here," the fourth jail keeper said, pointing.

"By God's eyelid, I should know his face!" the first jail keeper said. "It is Gill Cutpurse, the thief who was hanged this morning!"

"It is him!" Shackles said.

"The devil surely has a hand in this!" the second jail keeper said.

"What shall we do?" the third jail keeper said.

"Carry the news of it to the sheriffs," Shackles said.

"And to the Justices," the first jail keeper said.

"This is strange!" the fourth jail keeper said.

"And smells strongly of the devil!" the third jail keeper said.

"I have the sulphur of Hell-coal in my nose," the second jail keeper said.

"Phew!" the first jail keeper said.

"Carry him in," Shackles said.

"Let's go," the first jail keeper said.

"How rank it is!" the second jail keeper said.

They exited, carrying the body.

Sir Paul Eitherside, Merecraft, Everill, Trains, Fitzdottrel, Lady Eitherside, Lady Tailbush, Pitfall, Ambler, and some attendants had assembled in the courtroom. Fitzdottrel was lying in a bed.

Sir Paul Eitherside, who was the Justice, was wondering about and marveling at the case as the others told him about it.

"This is the most notable conspiracy that I ever heard of," Sir Paul Eitherside said.

Merecraft said, "Sir, they had given Fitzdottrel potions that made him fall in love with the counterfeit lady —"

Everill interrupted, "— right up to the time of the delivery of the deed —"

Merecraft interrupted, "— and then the witchcraft began to appear, for immediately he fell into his fit —"

Everill interrupted, "— of rage at first, sir, which since has much increased."

"Good Sir Paul," Lady Tailbush requested, "see Fitzdottrel, and punish the impostors."

"That is the reason for why I came here, madam," Sir Paul Eitherside said.

"Let Master Eitherside alone, madam," Lady Eitherside said. "He knows what to do."

"Do you hear?" Sir Paul Eitherside said. "Call in the constable; I will have him by us. He's the King's officer! And let's have some citizens of credible reputation by us! I'll discharge my conscience clearly. I'll perform my duty as according to my conscience."

"Yes, sir," Merecraft said.

An attendant exited to carry out Sir Paul Eitherside's orders.

Merecraft added, "And send for Fitzdottrel's wife."

"And for the two sorcerers, by any means necessary!" Everill said.

Another attendant exited.

"I thought one a true lady," Lady Tailbush said. "I would have sworn he was a lady."

She said to Lady Eitherside, "So did you, Lady Eitherside! You thought that he was a lady!"

"Yes, I did. I swear by that light, and I wish that I might never stir if I am lying, Lady Tailbush."

"And I thought that the other one was a civil gentleman," Lady Tailbush said.

"But, madam, you know what I told Your Ladyship," Everill said.

Manly had asked Everill to say nice things about him to Lady Tailbush when he was courting her, but instead Everill had said bad things about him.

"I now see the truth of it," Lady Tailbush said. "I was providing a banquet for them, after I had finished instructing the fellow De-vile, who was the gentleman's manservant."

"The fellow De-vile has been found to be a thief, madam," Merecraft said. "He robbed your usher Master Ambler this morning."

"What!" Lady Tailbush said.

"I'll tell you more soon," Merecraft said.

Fitzdottrel began to act as if he were having a fit.

He shouted, "Give me some garlic! Garlic! Garlic! Garlic!"

Garlic is supposed to be good at protecting oneself from demons.

"Listen to the poor gentleman," Merecraft said. "How he is tormented!"

"My wife is a whore," Fitzdottrel shouted at Sir Paul Eitherside. "I'll kiss her no more, and why? Mayn't thou be a cuckold, as well as I? Ha! Ha! Ha! Ha! Ha! Ha! Ha!"

Devils and cuckolds have horns.

Was Sir Paul Eitherside a cuckold? Perhaps. Earlier, when Wittipol was pretending to be the Spanish lady, Lady Eitherside had said, "As I am honest, Tailbush, I think that if nobody should love me but my poor husband, I would just hang myself."

Trying to understand the words and sounds, Sir Paul Eitherside said, "That is the devil who speaks and laughs in him."

"Do you think so, sir?" Merecraft asked.

"I discharge my conscience," Sir Paul Eitherside said. "On my conscience, I believe that."

"And isn't the devil good company?" Fitzdottrel shouted. "Yes, certainly."

As part of his "possession," Fitzdottrel was speaking at various times with different voices: that of a man, that of a woman, that of a child. More than one demon can possess a human being.

"How he changes, sir, his voice!" Everill said.

Of course, both Merecraft and Everill were trying to convince Sir Paul Eitherside — the Justice — that Fitzdottrel was bewitched.

Fitzdottrel shouted, "And a cuckold is wherever he puts his head with a vengeance if his horns are forth — the devil's companion! Look, look, look, else."

"How he foams at the mouth!" Merecraft said.

"And how his belly swells!" Everill said.

"Oh, me!" Lady Tailbush said. "What's that there, rising in his belly?"

The swelling resembled that of an erection.

"A strange thing!" Lady Eitherside said. "Hold it down."

Trains and Pitfall both said, "We cannot, madam."

"It is too apparent, this!" Sir Paul Eitherside said. "What I am seeing cannot be doubted."

Wittipol and Manly and Mrs. Frances Fitzdottrel entered the room.

"Wittipol!" Fitzdottrel cried. "Wittipol!"

"What is this?" Wittipol asked. "What play have we here?"

He knew immediately that Fitzdottrel was acting.

"What fine new matters?" Manly asked.

"*The Coxcomb and the Coverlet*," Wittipol said, making up a title for the "play."

A coxcomb is a fool. People who pretended to be bewitched covered themselves with a coverlet in order to hide their paraphernalia, such as bladders and bellows to make it appear that their belly was swelling.

"Oh, strange impudence!" Merecraft said. "That these should come to face their sin!"

He had been one of the people calling for them to be forced to come.

"And to outface — defy — justice and the Justice," Everill said. "They are the parties, sir. They are responsible for the witchcraft."

"Say nothing," Sir Paul Eitherside said.

"Did you notice, sir, upon their coming in, how Fitzdottrel called out 'Wittipol'?" Merecraft asked.

"And he never saw them come in," Everill said.

"I promise you that I did notice that," Sir Paul Eitherside said. "Let them play a while."

He wanted to see what would happen.

Fitzdottrel hummed, "Buzz! Buzz! Buzz! Buzz."

"It's a pity — the poor gentleman!" Lady Tailbush said. "How he is tortured!"

"For shame, Master Fitzdottrel!" his wife said, going over to him. "What do you mean by counterfeiting being bewitched like this?"

"Oh!" Fitzdottrel said. "Oh! She comes with a needle, and thrusts it in, she pulls out that, and she puts in a pin, and now, and now! I don't know how and I don't know where, but she pricks me here, and she pricks me there. Oh! Oh!"

Sir Paul Eitherside said to Mrs. Frances Fitzdottrel, "Woman, stop doing that!"

"What, sir?" Wittipol asked.

"A practice that is foul for one so fair," Sir Paul Eitherside said.

Wittipol asked Sir Paul Eitherside, "Do you really believe this playacting?"

Manly also asked Sir Paul Eitherside, "Do you believe in it?"

"Gentlemen, I'll discharge my conscience," Sir Paul Eitherside said. "This is clearly a conspiracy! A dark and devilish practice! I detest it!"

"The justice surely will prove to be the merrier man!" Wittipol said.

According to Wittipol, Sir Paul Eitherside was funnier and more to be laughed at than Fitzdottrel — Sir Paul was the bigger fool.

"This is very strange, sir," Wittipol said.

"Don't confront authority with impudence," Sir Paul Eitherside said. "I tell you, I detest it."

Gilthead and Sledge entered the room.

Sir Paul Eitherside said, "Here comes Sledge — the King's constable — and with him is a very honorable commoner and my good friend, Master Gilthead. I am glad that before such witnesses I can profess my conscience and my detestation of it. Horrible! Most unnatural! Abominable!"

He had misspoken: "I am glad that before such witnesses I can profess my conscience and my detestation of it" sounded as if he detested his conscience.

No doubt Wittipol and Manly did.

While the others were paying attention to the new arrivals, Merecraft and Everill advised Fitzdottrel.

Everill whispered to Fitzdottrel, "You do not contort your body enough."

Merecraft whispered to him, "Wallow! Gnash your teeth!"

Fitzdottrel redoubled his efforts.

"Oh, how he is vexed!" Lady Tailbush said.

"It is very manifest," Sir Paul Eitherside said.

Everill whispered to Merecraft, "Give him more soap to foam with."

He whispered to Fitzdottrel, "Now lie still."

Once Fitzdottrel stopped thrashing around in bed, Merecraft was able to secretly slip some soap to him.

Merecraft whispered, "And act a little."

Fitzdottrel began to mime smoking tobacco.

Lady Tailbush asked Sir Paul Eitherside, who had been interpreting Fitzdottrel's actions and words, "What is he doing now, sir?"

Sir Paul Eitherside said, "He is showing the taking of tobacco, with which the Devil is so delighted."

"Hum!" Fitzdottrel shouted.

"And he is calling for hum — strong ale," Sir Paul Eitherside said. "You takers of strong waters and tobacco, look closely at this."

Fitzdottrel shouted as he clapped his hands, "Yellow! Yellow! Yellow! Yellow!"

"That's yellow starch," Sir Paul Eitherside said. "The devil's the idol of that color. He ratifies it with clapping of his hands. The proofs are pregnant — they are convincing."

"How the devil can act!" Gilthead said.

"He is the master of actors, Master Gilthead, and of playwrights, too!" Sir Paul Eitherside said. "You heard him talk in rhyme! I forgot to mention it to you, a while ago."

Earlier, the play-acting Fitzdottrel had said, "My wife is a whore. I'll kiss her no more!"

He had also said, "She comes with a needle, and thrusts it in, she pulls out that, and she puts in a pin, and now, and now! I don't know how and I don't know where, but she pricks me here, and she pricks me there."

Fitzdottrel used the finely ground fibers he had put in a walnut shell to create a fireball.

"See, he spits fire," Lady Tailbush said.

"Oh, no! He plays at figgum," Sir Paul Eitherside said. "The devil is the author of wicked figgum."

A figgum is a juggler's trick.

Earlier, Fitzdottrel or Merecraft or Everill had prepared a walnut to enable him to spit fire. The walnut shell had been filled with a flammable substance that would enable him to appear to spit fire. For example, fire-breathers today may use cornstarch or alcohol. They put some in their mouth and then spray it over a small flame, producing a burst of fire.

Apparently, Sir Paul Eitherside had seen Fitzdottrel fill his mouth with the flammable substance in the walnut shell — finely ground sawdust or flour, perhaps? — and then seen him spray it over a lit candle, producing a burst of fire.

Rather than recognizing it as an impostor's trick, he interpreted it as a juggler's trick. Since "the devil is the author of wicked figgum," according to Sir Paul Eitherside, this was more evidence that Fitzdottrel was truly bewitched.

Manly asked Wittipol, "Why don't you speak to Sir Paul Eitherside?"

Manly thought that perhaps Wittipol could talk sense into him.

Wittipol replied, "If I had all innocence of man to be endangered, and he could save, or ruin it, I'd not breathe a syllable in request to such a fool as he makes himself."

Suppose Humankind was put on trial, and Sir Paul Eitherside was the judge who could save Humankind or have Humankind executed. Further suppose that Sir Paul Eitherside asked Wittipol to speak. Wittipol would say nothing to such a fool as Sir Paul Eitherside was making himself out to be.

Presumably, Wittipol would be OK with whatever decision Sir Paul Eitherside would make. If Humankind were judged innocent and so would survive, that would be OK with Wittipol; after all, good people such as Manly exist. If Humankind were judged guilty and so would be executed, that would be OK with Wittipol; after all, foolish people such as Fitzdottrel and Sir Paul Eitherside exist.

Or, perhaps, Wittipol would not be OK with whatever decision Sir Paul Eitherside would make. If Humankind were judged innocent and so would survive, that would not be OK with Wittipol; after all, foolish people such as Fitzdottrel and Sir Paul Eitherside exist. If Humankind were judged guilty and so would be executed, that would not be OK with Wittipol; after all, good people such as Manly exist.

"Oh, they whisper, whisper, whisper," Fitzdottrel said about Wittipol and Manly. "We shall have a score more of devils to come to dinner in me the sinner."

"Alas, poor gentleman!" Lady Eitherside said.

Sir Paul Eitherside said about Wittipol and Manly, "Separate them. Keep them each away from the other."

Wittipol would not talk to Sir Paul Eitherside, but Manly was willing.

"Are you insane, sir, or what grave foolishness moves you to take the side of so much villainy?" Manly asked Sir Paul Eitherside. "We are not afraid either of law or trial; let us be examined what our objectives were, what the means we had to work by, and the feasibility of those means. Do not make a decision against us before you hear us."

"I will not hear you," Sir Paul Eitherside said, "yet I will make a decision based on the circumstances."

The circumstances included circumstantial evidence.

"Will you do so, sir?" Manly asked.

"Yes, the circumstances are obvious," Sir Paul Eitherside said.

"Not as obvious as your folly!" Manly said.

"I will discharge my conscience, and do all things necessary to the meridian — the highest point — of justice," Sir Paul Eitherside said.

"You do well, sir," Gilthead said.

"Provide for me three or four dishes of good meat to eat," Fitzdottrel said. "I'll feast on them and their tricks; a Justice's head and brains shall be the first dish I will eat."

"The devil loves not justice," Sir Paul Eitherside said. "You may see that from the way the possessed man talks."

Fitzdottrel added, "Give me a spare rib of my wife, and a whore's innards! Give me a whole Gilthead."

Sir Paul Eitherside whispered to Gilthead, "Don't be troubled, sir; the devil speaks it."

The devil's speaking such a thing might very well trouble the person the devil was talking about.

Fitzdottrel shouted, "Yes, wis; knight, shite; Paul, jowl; owl, foul; troll, bowl."

He pronounced the words in such a way that each pair of words rhymed.

Sir Paul Eitherside said, "This is crambe, another of the devil's games!"

In the game of crambe, players had to come up with rhymes for a certain word.

Merecraft whispered to Fitzdottrel, "Speak, sir, some Greek, if you can."

The devil knows many languages; sinners speak many languages.

Merecraft then whispered to Everill, "Isn't the justice Sir Paul Eitherside a solemn gamester?"

For someone who regarded games as evil, the serious Sir Paul Eitherside certainly knew a lot about them.

"Quiet!" Everill whispered back.

Fitzdottrel said, "*Οἴμοι κακοδαίμων, Καὶ τρισκακοδαίμων, καὶ τετράκις, καὶ πεντάκις, καὶ δωδεκαικις, καὶ μυριακις.*"

Translated: "Alas! alas! I am a lost man. Ah! thrice, four, five, twelve times, or rather ten thousand times unhappy fate!"

Sir Paul Eitherside said, "He curses in Greek, I think."

Everill whispered to Fitzdottrel, "Use your Spanish that I taught you."

Fitzdottrel said, "*Quebrémos el ojo de burlas.*"

Fitzdottrel, who had learned the Spanish poorly, had said, "Let's break his eye in jest."

Everill tried to cover up the mistaken Spanish: "What? Your rest? Let's break his neck in jest, the devil says."

Fitzdottrel then said in Spanish, "*Di grátia, Signòr mio, se havete denári fataméne parte.*"

Translated: "If you please, sir, if you have money, give me some of it."

Merecraft said, "What! Would the devil borrow money?"

Fitzdottrel said in French, "*Oui, Oui, monsieur, un pauvre diable! Diabletin!*"

Translated: "Yes, yes, sir, a poor devil! A poor little devil!"

"It is the devil speaking, judging by his several languages," Sir Paul Eitherside said.

Carrying Ambler's possessions, Shackles, the jail keeper of Newgate Prison, entered the room, and asked, "Where's Sir Paul Eitherside?"

"Here I am," he said. "What's the matter?"

"Oh!" Shackles said. "Such an accident has happened at Newgate, sir. A great piece of the prison is torn down! The devil has been there, sir, in the body of the young cutpurse who was hanged this morning, but he was wearing new clothes, sir. Every one of us recognized him. These things were found in his pocket."

"Those are mine, sir," Ambler said.

"I think he was committed on your charge, sir, for a new felony," Shackles said.

"Yes," Ambler confirmed.

"He's gone, sir, now," Shackles said, "and left us the dead body. But he also left, sir, such an infernal stink and steam behind that you cannot see St. Pulchre's steeple yet. They smell the stink as far as the market town of Ware, as the wind lies by this time, I am sure."

St. Pulchre's steeple was the church of St. Sepulchre, which was close to Newgate Prison.

"Is this the truth, friend?" Fitzdottrel asked. "Do you give your word that it is true?"

"Sir, you may see it for yourself, and satisfy yourself that it is true," Shackles said.

Realizing that Pug — whom he called Devil, and who had told him that he had possessed the body of a cutpurse who was hanged this morning — really was a devil, Fitzdottrel immediately said, "Then it is time to stop counterfeiting that I am possessed."

He said to Sir Paul Eitherside, "Sir, I am not bewitched, nor do I have a devil inside me — no more than you do. I defy the devil by telling the truth, I do, and I admit I did abuse you with my counterfeiting.

"These two gentlemen — Merecraft and Everill — put me up to it. I have faith against the devil. These two gentlemen taught me all my tricks. I will tell the truth and shame the fiend. See here, sir, are my bellows, and my false belly, and my mouse that I would have pretended to come out of my mouth, and everything else that I would have pretended to have come out of my mouth!"

Manly said to Sir Paul Eitherside, "Sir, aren't you ashamed now of your solemn, serious vanity?"

"I will make honorable amends to truth," Sir Paul Eitherside said.

"And so will I," Fitzdottrel said. "But these two men — Wittipol and Manly — are still cheaters, and they have my land, as plotters with my wife, who, although she is not a witch, is worse — she is a whore!"

"Sir, you misrepresent her," Manly said. "She is chaste and virtuous, and we are honest men. I know of no glory a man would hope to acquire by proclaiming his own follies, but you'll still be an ass, in spite of providence and God's gifts."

He then said to Sir Paul Eitherside, "Please go in, sir, and hear the truth, and then judge these men, and make amends for your late rashness, when you shall hear about the pains and care that were taken to save from ruin this fool: his Grace of Drowned-land!"

"My land is drowned indeed," Fitzdottrel said.

"Be quiet!" Sir Paul Eitherside ordered Fitzdottrel.

Manly added, "And you shall hear how much his modest and too worthy wife has suffered being misunderstood by him; you will blush, first for your own belief in what you thought were her faults, but you will blush more for his actions.

"His land is his, and never, by my friend or by myself, was it meant to be put to any other use except to benefit her — his wife — who has equal right to the land. If any other had worse counsels regarding Fitzdottrel's land —"

Manly looked at Merecraft and Everill and said, "I know I speak to those who can understand me."

He then continued, "— let them repent their sins, and be not detected. It is not manly to take joy or pride in human errors; we all do ill things. They do them worst who love them, and dwell there until the plague comes. The few who have the seeds of goodness left will sooner make their way to a true life by shame, than by punishment."

APPENDIX A: THE PROLOGUE AND THE EPILOGUE

The Prologue (Original Language, Modern Spelling)

The Devil Is an Ass. That is today
    The name of what you are met for, a new play.
    Yet, grandees, would you were not come to grace
    Our matter with allowing us no place.
    Though you presume Satan a subtle thing,
    And may have heard he's worn in a thumb-ring,
    Do not on these presumptions force us act
    In compass of a cheese-trencher. This tract
    Will ne'er admit our vice because of yours —
    Anon, who, worse than you, the fault endures
    That yourselves make, when you will thrust and spurn,
    And knock us o' the elbows, and bid, turn;
    As if, when we had spoke, we must be gone,
    Or, till we speak, must all run in to one,
    Like the young adders at the old one's mouth?
    Would we could stand due north; or had no south,
    If that offend; or were Muscovy glass,
    That you might look our scenes through as they pass.
    We know not how to affect you. If you'll come
    To see new plays, pray you afford us room,
    And show this but the same face you have done
    Your dear delight, *The Devil of Edmonton.*
    Or if, for want of room, it must miscarry,
    'Twill be but justice that your censure tarry
    Till you give some. And when six times you ha' seen 't.
    If this play do not, the devil is in 't.

The Prologue (Modern English)

The Devil Is an Ass. That is today

The name of what you are met for, a new play.

Yet, grandees, I wish you had not come to grace

Our play by sitting on stools placed on the stage and cramping the acting space and allowing us no space to do our work.

Though you presume Satan a subtle thing,

And may have heard he's worn in a thumb-ring,

[Note: Some members of this society thought that familiar spirits — supernatural entities that assist witches, warlocks, etc. — were sometimes kept in a thumb-ring.]

Do not on these presumptions force us to act

In a space the size of a cheese-platter. This space

Will never admit our Vice because of yours —

Our Vice who, worse than you, soon endures the fault — the vice —

That you yourselves make, when you will thrust and kick,

And knock us on the elbows, and tell us to turn and when someone calls to you, you turn and face them;

As if, once we had spoken, we must be gone,

Or, until we speak, must all run in to one,

Like the young adders at the old one's mouth?

[The Prologue is complaining that the gallants on stage take up so much room that the actors have to leave unless they are delivering their lines — sometimes the gallants even push the actors away!

[The Prologue also is complaining that the vice of the audience — their bad behavior — will soon cause the Vice, a character in the play, to suffer.

[Note: This society believed that the mother adder would protect her young adders by letting them run in her mouth and down to her belly: a safe place. The actors who are pushed away have to gather together for protection.]

I wish we actors could stand due north and always face the audience; or had no south — no backs,

If that offend; or I wish that we actors were transparent like mica,

So that you might look through us at our scenes as we actors pass by in front of you people on stage.

We don't know how to influence you. If you'll come

To see new plays, please give us room to act,

And show this play just the same face you have shown to

Your dear delight, *The Devil of Edmonton*.

[Note: *The Merry Devil of Edmonton* was a popular play whose author is not known.]

Or if, for lack of room for us actors to act in, this play must miscarry and fail,

It will be but justice that you delay making a critical judgment

Until you give us some room. And when six times you have seen it,

If this play does not please you, the devil is in it.

The Epilogue

Thus the projector here is overthrown.
    But I have now a project of mine [my] own,
    If it may pass: that no man would invite
    The poet from us to sup forth tonight,
    If the play please. If it displeasant [unpleasant] be,
    We do presume that no man will; nor we.

***

Note: The actor who played Wittipol may speak the Epilogue. In it, he is saying that if the play is a success, he wishes that the audience members will not invite the playwright, Ben Jonson, to dine with them because the actors will want to treat him. But if the play is a failure, he presumes that the audience members will not invite the playwright, Ben Jonson, to dine with them — and neither will the actors.

APPENDIX B: NOTES

— 1.1 —

Satan says:

He ne'er will be admitted there where Vennor comes.

(1.1.94)

Source of Above: Jonson, Ben. *The Devil is an Ass.* Ed. Peter Happé. Manchester and New York: Manchester University Press, 1994. Page 63.

Below is the entry on "Richard Vennar" by Edward Irving Carlyle in the *Dictionary of National Biography*, Volume 88:

VENNAR or VENNARD, RICHARD (d. 1615?), author, was the younger son of John Vennar of Salisbury, a commissioner of the peace. He was educated by Adam Hill [q. v.], prebendary and succentor of Salisbury Cathedral, proceeding about 1572 to Balliol College, Oxford, where he studied for two years as a fellow commoner. He crossed to France towards the close of 1574, visited the court of Henri III, and procured letters of commendation to the emperor, Maximilian II. After some stay in Germany he returned home, and became a member of Barnard's Inn. He was admitted to Lincoln's Inn on 10 June 1581, receiving the privileges of a special admission on 25 July 1587 (Records of Lincoln's Inn, 1896, i. 93). On the death of his father he found himself involved in a lawsuit with the husband of his elder brother's widow for the possession of his patrimonial estates, and was ultimately compelled to take a younger brother's portion. In 1600 he proceeded to Scotland, and injudiciously solicited the intervention of James VI with the lords of the council. He had a favourable reception, and composed a thanksgiving for the delivery of James from the Gowrie conspiracy, which was presented to the king. His good reception aroused Elizabeth's anger, and on his return to England he was promptly arrested and imprisoned for a short time 'as a dangerous member to the state.' In 1601 appeared 'The Right Way to Heaven: and the true testimonie of a faithfull and loyall subject. Compiled by Richard Vennard of Lincolnes Inne. Printed by Thomas Este,' London, 4to, a work of a religious character, but abounding in adulation of Queen Elizabeth. The first part was reprinted in the following year with several alterations and additions, with the title, 'The Right Way to Heauen, and a good presedent for Lawyers and all other good Christians.' It was reprinted in Nichols's 'Progresses of Queen Elizabeth' (iii. 532–43). An undated reprint of the second part, 'The True Testimonie,' is preserved in the Bridgwater Library. It is prefaced by a dedication to James I, and contains a thanksgiving for the deliverance of the kingdom from the gunpowder plot (Collier, Cat. of Bridgwater Libr. p. 321). Not realising much by the sale, Vennar, who had in contemplation a second journey to Scotland, proclaimed his intention of representing England's triumphs over Spain in a masque entitled 'Englands Ioy.' The broadside of the plot is in possession of the Society of Antiquaries, and has been reprinted in their 'Miscellanies' (x. 196). He announced that it would be represented at the Swan on 6 Nov. 1602, and a large company, including many noblemen, assembled to witness it. After taking the entrance money, however, Vennar disappeared, and the audience revenged themselves by breaking up the furniture. Vennar himself states that he was arrested by bailiffs when the masque was about to begin, but Chamberlain relates that he fled on horseback, was pursued, captured, and brought before Sir John Popham, who treated the affair as a jest, and bound him over in five pounds to appear at the sessions (Chamberlain, Letters, Camden Soc. p. 163; Hazlitt, Shakespeare Jest Books, 1864, i. 145). The episode caused much amusement. Vennar was universally regarded as an impostor and dubbed 'England's Joy,' a name which gave him peculiar annoyance. In 1614 he wrote a vehement protest, entitled 'An Apology: written by Richard Vennar of Lincolnes Inne, abusively called Englands Joy. To represse the contagious ruptures of the infected multitude. ... London. Printed by Nicholas Okes.' The work is divided into two parts, of which the first is autobiographical, and the second relates Vennar's exertions to obtain the abolition of imprisonment for debt in England. The only perfect copy extant is in the British Museum Library, but it has been reprinted in Collier's 'Illustrations of Old English Literature' (vol. iii.). Collier inaccurately claims that it is the 'oldest piece of prose autobiography' in English. Several allusions to 'England's Joy' occur in contemporary literature, particularly in Ben Jonson's 'Love Restored' (1610–11), in his 'Masque of Augures' (1622), and in Sir John Suckling's comedy, 'The Goblins' (1646). A poem entitled 'Englands Joy,' commemorating the defeat of the Irish in 1600 under Hugh O'Neill, second earl of Tyrone [q. v.], by R. V., published without date, place, or printer's name, is sometimes attributed to Vennar, but may quite as well be the work of Richard Rowlands alias Verstegen [q. v.]

In 1606 Vennar was arrested on suspicion of an intention to defraud Sir John Spencer of 500l. on pretence of preparing a masque under the patronage of Sir John Watts [q. v.], the lord mayor. After that he avoided London, and lived chiefly in Essex and Kent. In spite of the exertions on behalf of debtors of which he speaks in his 'Apology,' Vennar himself perished before 1617 in 'the black hole' of Wood Street counter, in the most abject misery, the victim of his keeper's resentment (Fennor, Compters Commonwealth, 1617, p. 64). Taylor in his 'Cast over the Water. ... Given gratis to William Fennor, the Rimer,' 1615, accused one Fennor of passing off as his own some manuscripts in reality written by

> *Poor old Vennor, that plaine dealing man,*
> *Who acted Englands Ioy first at the Swan.*

Fennor's theft was probably committed while Vennar was confined in Wood Street counter. [Vennar's Works; Corser's Collectanea (Chetham Soc.), v. 323–32; Fleay's English Drama, ii. 265; Ritson's Bibliogr. Poetica, p. 380; Collier's Hist. of Dram. Poetry, iii. 321, 405; Collier's Bibliogr. Catalogue, ii. 466–9; Nichols's Progr. of James I, ii. 398, iii. 139; Dodsley's Collection of Old Plays, 1780, x. 72; Hazlitt's Handbook; Hazlitt's Collections and Notes, 1st ser.; Manningham's Diary (Camden Soc.), pp. 82, 93.]

Source of Above:

https://en.wikisource.org/wiki/Vennar,_Richard_(DNB00)

— 1.6 —

Fitzdottrel says:

Well, begin, sir,

There is your bound, sir. Not beyond that rush.

(1.6.72-73)

Source of Above: Jonson, Ben. *The Devil is an Ass*. Ed. Peter Happé. Manchester and New York: Manchester University Press, 1994. Page 83.

Many people think that loose rushes were strewn on the floor, but C. M Stone states that that makes no sense; instead, rush mats were placed on the floor:

What are rushes[1]? They're herbaceous plants that bare a superficial resemblance to grasses or sedges. Their leaves are typically rounded or flat. They grow in a wide variety of moisture conditions and have evergreen leaves, which would make them very useful for a fiber plant to gather year round for domestic purposes. The soft rush, called igusa *in Japanese, is woven as a covering for tatami mats. [...]*

The cloth Medieval Europeans were wearing was woven. The tapestries they hung on their walls were woven. The braids in long hair were woven. And yet many writers would have us believe that these people were so gross that they just threw rush leaves on the ground and walked on them instead of weaving mats? And while being this disgusting, they also had the sense to never display this unhygienic practice in any works of art? [...]

Fresh mats would be woven and laid down. Fragrant herbs were strewn on top so that when they were pressed between the foot and mat beneath they'd release their scent. (This same effect wouldn't work with a pile of loose rushes.) As the mats dried out (and can you imagine what a ridiculous fire hazard piles of loose rushes would be?), they'd absorb unpleasant odors from foot traffic and whatever was dropped on them. At the end of the season they'd be hauled out and replaced with new mats, bringing fresh scents and a clean floor once again. For special occasions, mats might be stacked up somewhere with storage, leaving clean and unworn floors for receiving company, which could then have decorative rugs instead. Removing

---

1.   *https://en.wikipedia.org/wiki/Juncaceae*

loose material every time you received company, on the other hand, would be a lengthy, labor-intensive project with a lot of bits always left behind. [...]

The thing that I find so baffling about the loose rushes myth authors keep repeating is the fact that medieval/apple matting is[2] not[3] some[4] obscure[5] secret[6]. It currently covers the floors in Elizabethan Hardwick Hall[7] and many other National Trust properties in the UK. You can go see it in the environment it would have been used in historically right now.

Source of Above: C.M. Stone, "Historical Inaccuracy: Rushes strewn on the floor." Ceeemstone.com. 20 May 2016. Accessed on 5 July 2019. <https://tinyurl.com/y2xxng97>.

However, rushes were also strewn on the floor as well as made into mats. *The Cottage Gardener* (1849) quotes Dr. Bulleyn, who was born early in the reign of King Henry VIII:

In speaking of Rushes, he [Dr. Bulleyn] gives us this incidental notice of the customs of his time : — "Of rushes growing in running streams there be great plenty round about the Isle of Ely, my native country, whereof the plain people make mats and horse-coliars of the greater rushes, and of the smaller they make lights or candles for the winter. Rushes that grow upon dry ground be good to strew in halls, chambers, and galleries, to walk upon, defending apparel, as trains of gowns and kirtles, from dust. Rushes be old courtiers, and when they be nothing worth then they be cast out of doors — so be many that do tread upon them."

Source of above: *The Cottage Gardener* (1849)

<https://tinyurl.com/y3l9a9qb>.

Thomas Dekkar's *Belman of London* has this passage:

The windows were spread with hearbs, the chimney drest up with greene boughs, and the floors strewed with bulrushes, as if some lasse were that morning to be married.

Source of Above:

---

2.   *http://www.thehousedirectory.com/categories/search/flooring-wall-tiles-and-rugs/natural-matting*

3.   *http://www.gardenista.com/posts/rush-floor-matting-aka-medieval-or-apple*

4.   *http://www.remodelista.com/products/english-rush-floor-matting/*

5.   *http://www.waveneyrush.co.uk/product-info.php?id=2882*

6.   *http://blog.mcgrath2.com/2015/07/rush-matting/*

7.   *http://www.nationaltrust.org.uk/hardwick-hall*

Quoted in Henry Tyrell, Esq., *The Doubtful Plays of Shakspeare: The doubtful plays of Shakspere: being all the dramas attributed to the muse of the world's great poet*. Revised from the Original Editions. London: London Print. and Pub. Co., [18—?] P. 321.

— **2.6** —

Manly sings an unidentified song in Act 2, Scene 6. Chances are, he sings the first stanza of Ben Jonson's "A Celebration of Charis: IV. Her Triumph" since Wittipol sings the last two stanzas later in the scene.

— 2.6 —

He grows more familiar in his courtship, plays with her paps, kisses her hands, &
c.

(Stage Direction Between 2.6.70 and 2.6.71)

Source of Above: Jonson, Ben. *The Devil is an Ass*. Ed. Peter Happé. Manchester and New York: Manchester University Press, 1994. Page 119.

He grew more familiar in his courtship and intimate accesses, playing with her breasts, kissing her hands, etc.

Source of Above: My retelling.

These are liberties indeed, but a critic named William Gifford commented, "Liberties very similar to these were, in the poet's [Jonson's] time, permitted by ladies, who would have started at being told that they had foregone all pretensions to delicacy."

Source of Gifford's Quotation: William Gifford, *The Works of Ben Jonson: With Notes Critical and Explanatory, and a Biographical Memoir Volume 5*. <https://tinyurl.com/yxqcpxfb>.

Recommended Reading (mostly about later centuries):

Tracey E. Robey, "There Was Never a Time When Western Society Wasn't Weird About Cleavage: Classical paintings and Hulu's Harlots have been lying to you." 21 December 2017

<https://tinyurl.com/y4l97xzu>.

Check Out:

"Category:Female nipples in art." Wiki Commons.

<https://tinyurl.com/y3c4vm5c>

— 3.4 —

Act 3, Scene 4 contains an in-joke. Dick Robinson was a famous boy actor who played the role of a woman in plays. After he grew up, he continued to act and played the role of a man in plays. Scholars think that he originated the role of Wittipol, so when Engine says that Dick Robinson and Wittipol are exactly the same height, he is telling the literal truth.

"Οἴμοι κακοδαίμων, Καὶ τρισκακοδαίμων, καὶ τετράκις, καὶ πεντά κις, καὶ δωδεκαικις, καὶ μυριακις."

(5.8.112-114)

Source of Above: Jonson, Ben. *The Devil is an Ass*. Ed. Peter Happé. Manchester and New York: Manchester University Press, 1994. Page 219.

This is a quotation from Aristophanes, *Plutus*, lines 850-852 in the original Greek.

Below are the full four lines of dialogue and the speaker:

Συκοφάντης

οἴμοι κακοδαίμων, ὡς ἀπόλωλα δείλαιος,

καὶ κακοδαίμων καὶ τετράκις καὶ πεντάκις

καὶ δωδεκάκις καὶ μυριάκις[1]: ἰοὺ[2] ἰού.

οὕτω πολυφόρῳ συγκέκραμαι δαίμονι.

Aristophanes, *Plutus*, lines 850-854 in the original Greek.

Aristophanes. *Aristophanes Comoediae*, ed. F.W. Hall and W.M. Geldart, vol. 2. F.W. Hall and W.M. Geldart. Oxford. Clarendon Press, Oxford. 1907.

<https://tinyurl.com/y45exnpz>

Below is an English translation of the Greek:

Informer

(before he sees Cario)

"Alas! alas! I am a lost man. Ah! thrice, four, five, twelve times, or rather ten thousand times unhappy fate! Why, why must fortune deal me such rough blows?"

Aristophanes. "Wealth." *The Complete Greek Drama*, vol. 2. Ed. Eugene O'Neill, Jr. New York. Random House. 1938.

<https://tinyurl.com/y5jrfsyq>

---

1. http://www.perseus.tufts.edu/hopper/
    morph?l=muria%2Fkis&la=greek&can=muria%2Fkis0&prior=kai\

2. http://www.perseus.tufts.edu/hopper/
    morph?l=i%29ou%5C&la=greek&can=i%29ou%5C0&prior=muria/kis

APPENDIX C: ABOUT THE AUTHOR

It was a dark and stormy night. Suddenly a cry rang out, and on a hot summer night in 1954, Josephine, wife of Carl Bruce, gave birth to a boy — me. Unfortunately, this young married couple allowed Reuben Saturday, Josephine's brother, to name their first-born. Reuben, aka "The Joker," decided that Bruce was a nice name, so he decided to name me Bruce Bruce. I have gone by my middle name — David — ever since.

Being named Bruce David Bruce hasn't been all bad. Bank tellers remember me very quickly, so I don't often have to show an ID. It can be fun in charades, also. When I was a counselor as a teenager at Camp Echoing Hills in Warsaw, Ohio, a fellow counselor gave the signs for "sounds like" and "two words," then she pointed to a bruise on her leg twice. Bruise Bruise? Oh yeah, Bruce Bruce is the answer!

Uncle Reuben, by the way, gave me a haircut when I was in kindergarten. He cut my hair short and shaved a small bald spot on the back of my head. My mother wouldn't let me go to school until the bald spot grew out again.

Of all my brothers and sisters (six in all), I am the only transplant to Athens, Ohio. I was born in Newark, Ohio, and have lived all around Southeastern Ohio. However, I moved to Athens to go to Ohio University and have never left.

At Ohio U, I never could make up my mind whether to major in English or Philosophy, so I got a bachelor's degree with a double major in both areas, then I added a Master of Arts degree in English and a Master of Arts degree in Philosophy. Yes, I have my MAMA degree.

Currently, and for a long time to come (I eat fruits and veggies), I am spending my retirement writing books such as *Nadia Comaneci: Perfect 10*, *The Funniest People in Comedy*, *Homer's* Iliad: *A Retelling in Prose*, and *William Shakespeare's* Hamlet: *A Retelling in Prose*.

By the way, my sister Brenda Kennedy writes romances such as *A New Beginning* and *Shattered Dreams*.

APPENDIX D: SOME BOOKS BY DAVID BRUCE

Retellings of a Classic Work of Literature

Arden of Faversham: A Retelling

Ben Jonson's The Alchemist: *A Retelling*

Ben Jonson's The Arraignment, or Poetaster: *A Retelling*

Ben Jonson's Bartholomew Fair: *A Retelling*

Ben Jonson's The Case is Altered: *A Retelling*

Ben Jonson's Catiline's Conspiracy: *A Retelling*

Ben Jonson's The Devil is an Ass: *A Retelling*

Ben Jonson's Epicene: *A Retelling*

Ben Jonson's Every Man in His Humor: *A Retelling*

Ben Jonson's Every Man Out of His Humor: *A Retelling*

Ben Jonson's The Fountain of Self-Love, or Cynthia's Revels: *A Retelling*

Ben Jonson's The Magnetic Lady, or Humors Reconciled: *A Retelling*

Ben Jonson's The New Inn, or The Light Heart: *A Retelling*

Ben Jonson's Sejanus' Fall: *A Retelling*

Ben Jonson's The Staple of News: *A Retelling*

Ben Jonson's A Tale of a Tub: *A Retelling*

Ben Jonson's Volpone, or the Fox: *A Retelling*

Christopher Marlowe's Complete Plays: Retellings

Christopher Marlowe's Dido, Queen of Carthage: *A Retelling*

Christopher Marlowe's Doctor Faustus: *Retellings of the 1604 A-Text and of the 1616 B-Text*

Christopher Marlowe's Edward II: *A Retelling*

Christopher Marlowe's The Massacre at Paris: *A Retelling*

Christopher Marlowe's The Rich Jew of Malta: *A Retelling*

Christopher Marlowe's Tamburlaine, Parts 1 and 2: *Retellings*

Dante's Divine Comedy: *A Retelling in Prose*

Dante's Inferno: *A Retelling in Prose*

Dante's Purgatory: *A Retelling in Prose*

Dante's Paradise: *A Retelling in Prose*

The Famous Victories of Henry V: *A Retelling*

From the Iliad *to the* Odyssey: *A Retelling in Prose of Quintus of Smyrna's* Posthomerica

George Chapman, Ben Jonson, and John Marston's Eastward Ho! *A Retelling*

George Peele's The Arraignment of Paris: *A Retelling*

George Peele's The Battle of Alcazar: *A Retelling*

George's Peele's David and Bathsheba, and the Tragedy of Absalom: *A Retelling*

George Peele's Edward I: *A Retelling*

George Peele's The Old Wives' Tale: *A Retelling*

George-a-Greene: *A Retelling*

The History of King Leir: *A Retelling*

Homer's Iliad: *A Retelling in Prose*

Homer's Odyssey: *A Retelling in Prose*

J.W. Gent.'s The Valiant Scot: *A Retelling*

Jason and the Argonauts: A Retelling in Prose of Apollonius of Rhodes' Argonautica

John Ford: Eight Plays Translated into Modern English

John Ford's The Broken Heart: *A Retelling*

John Ford's The Fancies, Chaste and Noble: *A Retelling*

John Ford's The Lady's Trial: *A Retelling*

John Ford's The Lover's Melancholy: *A Retelling*

John Ford's Love's Sacrifice: *A Retelling*

John Ford's Perkin Warbeck: *A Retelling*

John Ford's The Queen: *A Retelling*

John Ford's 'Tis Pity She's a Whore: *A Retelling*

John Lyly's Campaspe: *A Retelling*

John Lyly's Endymion, The Man in the Moon: *A Retelling*

John Lyly's Galatea: *A Retelling*

John Lyly's Love's Metamorphosis: *A Retelling*

John Lyly's Midas: *A Retelling*

John Lyly's Mother Bombie: *A Retelling*

John Lyly's Sappho and Phao: *A Retelling*

John Lyly's The Woman in the Moon: *A Retelling*

John Webster's The White Devil: *A Retelling*

King Edward III: *A Retelling*

Mankind: *A Medieval Morality Play* (A Retelling)

Margaret Cavendish's The Unnatural Tragedy: *A Retelling*

The Merry Devil of Edmonton: *A Retelling*

The Summoning of Everyman: *A Medieval Morality Play* (A Retelling)

Robert Greene's Friar Bacon and Friar Bungay: *A Retelling*

The Taming of a Shrew: *A Retelling*

Tarlton's Jests: A Retelling

Thomas Middleton's A Chaste Maid in Cheapside: *A Retelling*

Thomas Middleton's Women Beware Women: *A Retelling*

Thomas Middleton and Thomas Dekker's The Roaring Girl: *A Retelling*

Thomas Middleton and William Rowley's The Changeling: *A Retelling*

The Trojan War and Its Aftermath: Four Ancient Epic Poems

Virgil's Aeneid: *A Retelling in Prose*

William Shakespeare's 5 Late Romances: Retellings in Prose

William Shakespeare's 10 Histories: Retellings in Prose

William Shakespeare's 11 Tragedies: Retellings in Prose

William Shakespeare's 12 Comedies: Retellings in Prose

William Shakespeare's 38 Plays: Retellings in Prose

William Shakespeare's 1 Henry IV, aka Henry IV, Part 1: A Retelling in Prose

William Shakespeare's 2 Henry IV, aka Henry IV, Part 2: A Retelling in Prose

William Shakespeare's 1 Henry VI, aka Henry VI, Part 1: A Retelling in Prose

William Shakespeare's 2 Henry VI, aka Henry VI, Part 2: A Retelling in Prose

William Shakespeare's 3 Henry VI, aka Henry VI, Part 3: A Retelling in Prose

William Shakespeare's All's Well that Ends Well: A Retelling in Prose

William Shakespeare's Antony and Cleopatra: A Retelling in Prose

William Shakespeare's As You Like It: A Retelling in Prose

William Shakespeare's The Comedy of Errors: A Retelling in Prose

William Shakespeare's Coriolanus: A Retelling in Prose

William Shakespeare's Cymbeline: A Retelling in Prose

William Shakespeare's Hamlet: A Retelling in Prose

William Shakespeare's Henry V: A Retelling in Prose

William Shakespeare's Henry VIII: A Retelling in Prose

William Shakespeare's Julius Caesar: A Retelling in Prose

William Shakespeare's King John: A Retelling in Prose

William Shakespeare's King Lear: A Retelling in Prose

William Shakespeare's Love's Labor's Lost: A Retelling in Prose

William Shakespeare's Macbeth: A Retelling in Prose

William Shakespeare's Measure for Measure: A Retelling in Prose

William Shakespeare's The Merchant of Venice: A Retelling in Prose

William Shakespeare's The Merry Wives of Windsor: A Retelling in Prose

William Shakespeare's A Midsummer Night's Dream: A Retelling in Prose

William Shakespeare's Much Ado About Nothing: A Retelling in Prose

William Shakespeare's Othello: A Retelling in Prose

William Shakespeare's Pericles, Prince of Tyre: A Retelling in Prose

William Shakespeare's Richard II: A Retelling in Prose

William Shakespeare's Richard III: A Retelling in Prose

William Shakespeare's Romeo and Juliet: A Retelling in Prose

William Shakespeare's The Taming of the Shrew: A Retelling in Prose

William Shakespeare's The Tempest: A Retelling in Prose

William Shakespeare's Timon of Athens: A Retelling in Prose

William Shakespeare's Titus Andronicus: A Retelling in Prose

William Shakespeare's Troilus and Cressida: A Retelling in Prose

William Shakespeare's Twelfth Night: A Retelling in Prose

William Shakespeare's The Two Gentlemen of Verona: A Retelling in Prose

William Shakespeare's The Two Noble Kinsmen: A Retelling in Prose

William Shakespeare's The Winter's Tale: A Retelling in Prose